PSYCHIATRIC NURSE

Fern Shepard

Nurse Tracy Ross had many reasons for going home. Her mother needed her . . . and she needed a rest from the terrible strain she had been under. But she soon came to the shocking realization that you *can't* go home again. For back in her home town she found herself working with a doctor with whom she had once been violently in love . . . but even more difficult was the terrible secret she carried in her heart. Unable to reveal it, she knew that if she kept it hidden, many lives were doomed to tragedy.

OTHER LARGE PRINT BOOKS
BY
FERN SHEPARD

College Nurse
Sacrifice For Love
Rejected Love
Nurse Kitty's Secret

PSYCHIATRIC NURSE

Fern Shepard

Curley Publishing, Inc.
South Yarmouth, Ma.

Library of Congress Cataloging-in-Publication Data

Shepard, Fern, 1896–
  Psychiatric nurse / Fern Shepard.
    p. cm.
  ISBN 0–7927–0678–1 (lg. print). — ISBN 0–7927–0679–X (pbk. : lg.
  print)
    1. Large type books. I. Title.
  [PS3537.T9246P77 1991]
  813′.54—dc20   90–39541
                                                         CIP

Copyright © 1967 by Arcadia House

Published in Large Print by arrangement with Donald MacCampbell, Inc. in the United States, Canada, the U.K. and British Commonwealth and the rest of the world market.

Distributed in Great Britain, Ireland and the Commonwealth by CHIVERS LIBRARY SERVICES LIMITED, Bath BA1 3HB, England.

Printed in Great Britain

PSYCHIATRIC NURSE

Chapter One

The little girl on the bed was sobbing quietly and hopelessly when Tracy Ross went into the hospital room that October morning.

"What's the use washing me?" quavered the tremulous voice as Tracy took a cool wet cloth to the hot, thin little face. "I'm gonna die 'most any minute. And then I'll start burning up in a fire that won't ever go out."

Terror came alive in the child's big dark eyes. The small, wasted body trembled with fear as Tracy sat on the bed and drew the girl close in her arms.

"Whatever put all this nonsense in your head?"

Tracy's voice was light, with a hint of amusement. This was simply pretense, however. Inside, she was at a slow boil which rapidly quickened.

It was perfectly true that Leah Ormsby, a victim of leukemia, had only, at the most, a few more weeks to live. But you didn't tell a seven-year-old child that she was doomed.

What kind of a fiend would have said such a ghastly, outrageous thing?

Leah was a darling little girl, with the

1

sweetest smile. And there was a trusting, pleading expression in those enormous dark eyes that tore at Tracy's heart.

Generally speaking, Tracy's record as an R.N. was an enviable one. She had trained as a psychiatric nurse and specialized in that field in a mental institution in New York. Then, returning to this small southern town where she had grown up, she had taken over the charge of the children's section in the town's recently built, small but modern hospital.

During the brief time she had been there, only a few months, she had fallen in love with this line of work. Her love for children was instinctive, as was her gift at handling them. But she had one weakness, if you wanted to call it a weakness.

It was quite impossible for Tracy to follow one of the basic rules laid down for a nurse: Never become emotionally involved with the patient!

Now she held Leah's pitifully thin body close. She felt the trembling little arms around her neck, the tear-stained face pressed against her. And she knew an anger past all telling as the childish voice told her:

"I've got an awful disease, and I'll die pretty soon. 'Most any day now, I guess." A small, deep, hopeless sigh before the whispered words went on. "And after I'm dead, I'll go to hell and keep burning and burning. 'Cause that's what happens to wicked little girls like me. And oh, Tracy, I'm so scared, so awfully scared." Again the sigh, followed by a fresh outburst of tears.

Inwardly Tracy was seething. But for the child's sake she must control her anger, try to hide it with a pretense of a smile.

Pushing the child gently out of her arms, she propped pillows behind her back, smoothed back her blondish hair and gave her a sip of cold water.

"Now," she said, "I want to know who has been telling you all this rubbish! I'm sure it wasn't your mother. She wouldn't tell you cruel lies."

Neither, she added, would Dr. Sizer. "So who was it?"

"You mean –" the small voice hesitated, torn between a wistful hope and the great, dark terror – "it's a lie about me going to die?"

Choosing her words carefully, Tracy said gently: "Only God could give you a yes or no answer to that, honey. You have been a very sick little girl. But we're all doing our best to make you well again. What's more –" she smiled, again pushing the fair hair back from the feverish forehead – "you've got a lot

3

of prayers going for you. Your parents and all your friends and Dr. Sizer and myself – all are asking God to help us cure you. And believe me, sweetheart, prayer can work a real miracle."

Leah considered, with frowning concentration. "I got to have a miracle, you mean. Or else I'll die."

Frowning, Tracy returned to the more practical question. "You still haven't told me who said these awful things to you, Leah?"

"Miss Wilson," came the answer.

Fern Wilson.

Too choked with anger to risk speaking, Tracy got up, rearranged a blind to shut out the glare, then busied her fingers rearranging flowers in a vase.

Meanwhile, her riotous thoughts concentrated on Fern Wilson, the beautiful blonde girl who did volunteer work at the hospital. Her specialty was visiting with the children, bringing them toys, reading to them, telling them stories.

Stories about burning in hell, thought Tracy, inwardly gritting her teeth. But what can I do about it? She could, of course, tell all that she knew about the beauteous Miss Wilson. And she knew plenty. Oh, did she ever know the carefully hidden secret which no one else in this town knew!

4

However, what good would telling do? Maybe no good at all. For Dr. Bert Brooks was madly in love with Fern. And Dr. Brooks was chief of staff. It was doubtful if he would believe a word against the entrancing creature who, according to town gossip, had him so completely fascinated he no longer knew his head from his heels.

That was one problem she was up against. But there was another. *As a nurse, had she the ethical right to tell what she knew?*

The problem was a terrific one. Ever since her return to Oakwood, it had been haunting Tracy, like a ghost which refused to stay dead.

Forget it, she kept telling herself. Don't talk out of turn. Even if you don't happen to fancy Fern Wilson as a person, *give her a break.* This was a sensible line of reasoning, and it had helped – until the previous Sunday night.

That was the night which would always be remembered in the obscure little Southern town as the night of the awful fire.

Acres of valuable timberland had been destroyed; and before the blaze, out of control, had crept to within a few hundred feet of the hospital. Trapped by a sudden change in the wind, several volunteer firemen had been critically burned and rushed to the hospital. One had since died.

What or who had started the fire?

Everyone in the hospital, in the whole town was asking that question.

Everyone had his or her own pet theory, but no one knew the answer.

She went back to the bed.

"Now Leah, honey –" she began, only to have the child come up with the question that was torturing her seven-year-old mind.

"What's dying like, Tracy? Does it hurt awful bad?"

Before Tracy could formulate the right, comforting words, the door opened.

Turning, she saw Dr. Sizer coming in. He was a tall, slim, soft-spoken man with fine, deep-set gray eyes and an indefinable charm. Although she scarcely knew him, Tracy felt herself curiously attracted to him. Conjecturing as to why, she decided it was because he was so wonderfully gentle and understanding with Leah.

With a friendly but quite impersonal smile and good morning for Tracy, he went to the bed and took over with his little patient. "How's my little doll doing this morning?" he wanted to know, producing a lollypop instead of a stethoscope.

Then, noting the teary eyes, he wanted to know what the tears were all about, and

6

managed to elicit a giggle from Leah by asking very seriously: "Your boy friend stand you up, young lady?"

Tracy, escaping to the adjoining lavatory, splashed cold water over her eyes, straightened the cap on her inky black hair, then stood for a moment studying the familiar face which looked back at her. Slowly she shook her head, as if she found her reflection extremely depressing.

She was not, she was well aware, a born beauty contest winner. On the other hand, at its best she didn't consider her face too bad. She couldn't help knowing that she possessed very beautiful eyes, because so many had said so. Doctors, patients, friends – all the way from Virginia to New York, then back to Virginia again – all had been known to tell her: "You have the deepest blue eyes I've ever seen. They are truly beautiful, honestly." Or words to that effect.

But on this particular morning her eyes were shadowed by deep, dark circles, and her face looked pale and strained. "It's because of the pressure I've been under this last week," she decided.

Ever since the night of the fire, she had been working two shifts a day, once around the clock with brief periods out to catch an hour's sleep.

7

Oh, it had been rough, no doubt about that. The hospital, already filled to capacity, then had to care for all the fire victims.

But she wasn't the only one. All of the other pitifully new R.N.s had been pushed to the point of exhaustion, hadn't they? And did any of the others look like death warmed over? No.

With a sigh she sat down on the small lavatory stool, pushed at her hair, and tried to face the root of her trouble. If I don't stop thinking about it, Tracy decided, my poor brain will explode. And she got up, took another brief, dejected glance at the mirror and went back to her patient.

She found the doctor seated in an easy chair with Leah on his lap. Obviously he had performed a minor miracle. All the tears were gone. In their place was the loveliest smile. The child was gazing up at him with her heart in her eyes. And the doctor was saying:

"Sure you're going to die one of these days, kid. So is everybody else. So what? If that's all that's bugging you, forget it. There isn't anything bad to what folks call dying."

"Honest?" asked the small voice, filled with complete trust.

"Honest. Cross my heart and hope to die." The doctor grinned down at her. "Why, heck, you'll just fall asleep, same as you do

8

every night, and when you wake up you'll be in the most beautiful place you ever saw. There'll be flowers blooming, birds singing, all sort of marvelous colors, and you'll be all well and strong again."

"Will I be able to run and play with other little girls?" asked the child, who had been frail and sickly since birth, never up to normal fun and games.

"No doubt about it, honey. Any old darned thing you want to do, you can do. You'll have a whale of a time."

The small sigh held peace and contentment, as the fair head cuddled against the doctor's shoulder. "I guess dying ain't so bad. You make it sound like fun."

What a doctor! marveled Tracy, following Larry Sizer out to the corridor a few minutes later.

What a sweet, sweet guy!

Chapter Two

In the corridor, rubber-tired carts whispered briskly along, guided by harassed-looking aides. Two doors down, a wiry, red-haired R.N. preceded the white-jacketed doctor into the room where an asthma patient could be heard gasping for breath. Tracy stood waiting for the doctor's instructions.

They came swiftly, his tone curt, threaded with suppressed indignation. It was scarcely recognizable as the gentle, somehow hypnotic voice which had brought peace and comfort to the terrified child.

"That Wilson girl is to be kept out of this room, Nurse. Under no circumstances is she to be allowed to visit with Leah. Is that clear?"

"Yes, Doctor."

But, Tracy mused aloud, suppose Dr. Brooks undertook to countermand that order? A wry little smile twisted her lips. "He has been known to refer to Fern Wilson as an Angel of Mercy."

"Some angel!" snapped Larry Sizer, momentarily discarding professional reticence and expressing himself as a thoroughly angry man.

If Bert Brooks, as chief of staff, chose to let that loose-tongued blonde run loose among the other patients, that was his business.

"I don't happen to share his infatuation with a pretty face." A remark which needed no elaboration. The sizzling romance between the hospital head and the golden-haired volunteer worker was not only common knowledge in the hospital; it was the talk of the town.

"Neither am I a member of the hospital staff." Another statement which scarcely needed to be made.

Dr. Larry Sizer was a newcomer in town. Although his credentials were excellent, the town was divided in its opinion as to whether the man should be allowed to practice medicine.

It was known that he used hypnosis in the treatment of some cases. According to some of the old-timers, a hypnotist – any hypnotist, even if he did have a medical degree – was a charlatan and a fake; a dangerous fellow, to say the least.

Unbelievably – at least Tracy considered it unbelievable – there were a few modern doctors who more or less shared this opinion. Dr. Bert Brooks was one of them. He could not deny Larry the use of the hospital for any individual patient, but he could see to it that Larry was not invited to serve on the staff.

"But," Larry was saying, "I give the orders concerning my own patient. That means Leah. When I think," he went on furiously, "of that idiot blonde scaring the wits out of a sick little kid –" He shook his head. "Is she nuts?"

The question startled Tracy more than she

11

dared let on. "Could be," she said, smiling a small smile.

Then, even more startled, in a different way, she felt his hands on her arms.

A nurse passing along the corridor gave her a smile and a wink, as much as if to say: "Cheers for you, honey. Making a little headway with our woman-hater?"

Translated, that meant simply that Larry Sizer had never been known to date a girl during the slightly more than a year he had been in Oakwood, although quite a few girls, including some of the nurses and aides, had launched a determined campaign.

Larry was studying her face. "What's bugging you?" he asked. "You look ready to crack up."

Tracy smiled noncommittally. "Just tired, I guess."

"Tired?" He considered that, then shook his head. "You look more like a girl with a monkey on her back."

For heaven's sake, thought Tracy, was the man psychic?

"Well –" a comforting pat on her shoulder – "we all have our problems and worries."

He could, he went on, give her a shot to help that tired feeling. But he was a man who believed in getting at the cause, not the symptoms. There were times when talking

12

things out with an understanding friend could relieve tiredness better than all the drugs in the pharmacopoeia. If, by chance, she needed such a friend, consider him her boy.

He smiled at her, but his eyes were grave. "I have a good listening ear," he said, "and I keep office hours around the clock."

Feeling slightly dazed, Tracy watched him stride away. Was the man a mind-reader as well as a hypnotist? How could he have guessed that she had a problem which was worrying her sick?

She turned and went toward the ward, where she was busy for the next hour. But as she took temperatures, sponged feverish little bodies, filled out a series of charts, she kept thinking about Larry Sizer, and about his grave, penetrating gray eyes, and how he had seemed, for a moment or two, deeply concerned about her.

It was a singularly pleasant thought. Her mind played with it for a moment. Then she called a halt. "Pull yourself together, Tracy!"

The doctor's professional eye had spotted her as a girl who was mentally upset. Nothing strange about that, nor about his offering his services in case she needed advice. Nothing to any of it except the friendly gesture of a man who took the psychosomatic approach to illness, and believed in coping with mental problems before they got out of hand. Certainly there was nothing personal about anything he had said. Still, there had been a certain warmth in his voice, hadn't there, and an inexplicable *something* in his eyes meeting hers?

Oh, forget it! Her imagination must be working overtime. Anyway, she had no personal interest in Dr. Larry Sizer. Had she?

Tracy not only looked like an ill girl that morning; she also felt all the signs of a virus cold coming on. The morning passed, but her miserable feeling did not pass. Shortly before noon, she knew she would have to give up, go home, and catch up on some of the sleep she had lost this last week.

Arranging for a replacement to take over that afternoon, she was on her way out of the hospital when she thought of Martha Renard.

If I don't drop in for a few minutes and say hello, she thought, the old darling's feelings will be hurt.

She took the elevator back to the second floor.

Martha, aged ninety-three, was a terminal heart case. And she wanted no nonsense from the doctors about being good for another eight or ten years. She submitted to their pills, their cheery smiles and bedside manners. But they

14

couldn't fool her. She regarded the medical experts as a kind of necessary evil which helpless humans had to put up with. But she didn't and never had believed they knew what they were talking about much of the time. Even when they did know, they lied. They were just full of cheery little lies for an old woman like herself, regarding her, no doubt, as a senile old relic.

When Tracy entered her room that day, Martha was propped up against three or four pillows. She was wearing a shocking-pink satin bed jacket, an astonishing white wig (to hide her baldness) and, as always, she glittered with diamonds.

She was also wearing a glowering scowl as she snapped at Tracy: "You silly girl, if you don't stop wasting your time and energy traipsing in to see me every chance you get, I suppose you know what folks will be saying. Don't you?"

"What will they be saying, darling?" Tracy walked to the bed, gave her old friend a smile, a hug and a kiss, and sat on the edge of the bed.

She held out her package of cigarettes. "Want one?"

"Of course I want one." Martha reached greedily for one of the cigarettes, which were strictly forbidden. Doctor's orders – and just another little item to which she paid no attention.

After one or two jerky puffs, she announced, "That you're just another scheming nurse, making a great fuss over a rich old woman in her dotage, hoping to be remembered in my will. That's what they'll say."

Martha was the town's millionairess.

Tracy grinned. "Maybe they'll be right. Who knows?"

Now that that was all settled – "How's our famous southern beauty doing this morning?"

"Awful," snapped Martha, who, in actual fact, at one time had been a famous beauty.

There was nothing she liked better than to talk about the days, long, long ago, when she had been the toast of Richmond, with beautiful clothes galore, sweethearts galore, and diamonds galore. Her adoring papa had seen to it that each and every birthday brought with it a gorgeous diamond pin, or ring, or earrings. Once she was married, Ned, the handsome husband who had worshipped the ground she walked on, had taken up where papa left off.

But now, always with a deep, sorrowful sigh, she was just a withered old woman who had lived too long.

The sweethearts were gone, papa was gone,

her beloved Ned was gone. All she had left were her memories – and her beloved diamonds.

"I never knew," she was saying dismally, "that a body could have so many aches and pains."

She hadn't the strength to struggle out of the horrible hospital bed and stand up. When she did manage to crawl out, her silly old legs felt exactly like rubbery spaghetti. "What's more, they creak."

Tracy laughed. "Maybe they need a touch of salad oil," she teased.

"What they need," snapped the tart voice, "is to take off about fifty years of age."

Then the voice softened wonderfully, and her dark eyes, still bright despite her age, were filled with warmth and love as she caught Tracy's hand.

"Child, I'm just an old woman who's done for. Every night when I fall off to sleep, I know it's likely to be my last sleep. And to tell the truth, it can't come too soon to suit me. There's nothing to living when the world you knew and the ones you loved are all gone."

She paused, demanded another cigarette from Tracy, thought for a moment, then shook her head firmly. "When you've run your course, it's time to go. You remember that, honey. And don't ever let some fool of a

17

doctor tell you different."

"You don't mind dying?"

Another vigorous shake of the white head. "Not in the least." Then, adding one slight correction, she said wistfully: "Only thing I mind is going away and leaving all my lovely diamonds." She had, she said, always so adored beautiful, sparkling diamonds.

Tracy smiled, holding one small old hand in hers. "Well, here's a thought to cheer you up, Sweetie. There are those who believe when we die we go on to a place where there are jewels more dazzling than any we have here."

"Really?" Martha chuckled. "Now wouldn't that be nice."

"So even if you can't take any of these with you –" Tracy touched the blazing diamond on the hand she held. It was the most beautiful stone she had ever seen.

"You like that one?" Martha was watching her.

Suddenly, impulsively, the old lady pulled off the ring and placed it in Tracy's palm. "It's yours, Tracy. Wear it to remember a vain, silly, useless old woman who always loved you very dearly."

"I couldn't take it, Martha." Tears swam into Tracy's eyes, not only because of the offered ring, but also because of a thousand

18

remembered kindnesses.

Behind her bluster and tart mannerisms, Martha had a warm, great, generous heart.

Since childhood, Tracy had been a favorite with the old lady, who had never had children of her own. "I'm sure your mother can share just a little part of you for me to love," Martha had once said. That was the time she had brought Tracy the exquisite talking doll from Paris.

And there had been the time she had given Tracy the most beautiful birthday party any nine-year-old child ever had, with a check for a thousand dollars tucked in the white leather purse, because Tracy's dad was seriously ill at the time and her mother was finding it difficult to pay the bills which poured in.

"You were always so good to me, so kind," Tracy said, brushing away her tears. "But this ring – I can't accept it, darling. How can I?"

"Oh, stop all that foolish emoting, for heaven's sake." The voice was brusque, the old eyes teary. Maybe from time to time she had offered a few little gifts. Sheer selfishness on her part, actually, since she only gave because it gave her pleasure to do it.

"And I want no more nonsense from you about this ring, Tracy. If you refuse it, you'll make me extremely upset; likely as not bring on another heart attack that may finish me.

19

You wouldn't want that on your conscience, would you?"

When Tracy left the room, she was wearing the magnificent diamond. She had never owned such a valuable piece of jewelry, ever expected to. Already she felt great pride in it.

But she was a little frightened, too. The ring was worth a small fortune. Suppose anything were to happen to it?

Chapter Three

Leaving the old lady's room, again Tracy was aware of a headachy, slightly dizzy feeling. On her way to the parking lot and her small car, she inhaled some good deep breaths. The crisp autumn air drawn into her lungs made her feel slightly better. She decided to take the long way around, driving home. The mountain scenery was so gorgeous right now, it seemed a shame not to enjoy it when she had the chance.

As she drove, she kept glancing at the sparkling stone on her hand which held the wheel. Never had she expected to own such a beautiful ring. For a moment she thought only of the wonder of it. Then her worries came creeping back.

She headed the car along a winding highway which gave a panoramic view of the tapestry-colored hills, then back into town and onto Lee Avenue.

This was the ultra-fashionable street of Oakwood. It was the area where the people with money had their modern homes, their terraced gardens, their swimming pools.

It was also the street where Dr. Bert Brooks lived with his daughter, Cathy, his housekeeper, and his private office in the addition built onto the south end of his nine-room, two-story house.

As Tracy approached the house, she slowed down, a thoughtful look in her eyes. Both the slowing down and the faintly dreamy expression were automatic. She was never able to pass the house without recalling how, as a child, she had imagined herself madly in love with the handsome young medical student.

She thought, too, of the tears she had wept when she learned he was going to marry the pretty young schoolteacher. What a silly little fool I was, she thought now, just as the bulky figure of Mrs. Annie Barker came hurrying down the flagstone path which led up to the house.

Mrs. Barker was Bert's housekeeper.

Waving to Tracy to stop, she came over to the car, a kindly-faced woman wearing, at the moment, a fierce scowl.

"I saw your car coming, Tracy, and I was never so glad to see anybody in my life." She leaned against the car door, propping her arms on the ledge. "I need help." To be more exact, that poor child, Cathy, needed help.

"What's the problem, Annie?" asked Tracy, who knew the woman well, just as she knew almost everyone in this town where she had been born and lived until she went away to take her nurse's training.

"The poor child is upstairs in her room, crying her eyes out." Annie looked about to cry herself, from indignation. "Her father wouldn't let her go to school today. Said she was to stay in her room. That's supposed to be punishment for lying."

"Did she lie?"

"Cathy says not, and I believe her."

"Children do, sometimes," said Tracy carefully. She knew that Annie was inclined to be biased where Bert's little daughter was concerned. A terrifically maternal woman, she had taken Cathy to her heart following her mother's tragic death from an accidental fall on an icy pavement.

"Oh, sure. I used to tell lies myself when I

22

was a little kid. Harmless little lies. But this is different."

This, said Annie Barker darkly, was just part of the same old plot. "And you needn't smile like that, Tracy Ross, as if you took me for a senile old woman who had lost her wits."

As sure as you were born, that Fern Wilson was set on turning Bert against his own child. She was forever laying the blame on Cathy for things the child swore she hadn't done. The truth of it was, she wanted to get rid of the child before she married Bert. That baby-faced blonde was the kind who wouldn't want to be bothered with a step-daughter.

Fern Wilson again.

Wherever she turned, thought Tracy, that name popped up. Simultaneously, back popped her own worried doubts. But what could she do?

As if you didn't know what you should do! That was her little inner voice chiding her, advising her. You should go straight to Bert Brooks and tell him the whole story!

Only she couldn't. For one thing, there was the little matter of professional ethics involved.

Also, Bert would probably give a scornful laugh for her pains, refusing to believe a word she said.

When had an infatuated widower ever been

known to believe a word against the idol of his romantic, thirtyish, seriously bewitched dreams?

Annie Barker was still talking, and she truly seemed to be worried half sick. The trouble this morning, she said, was because of the unframed photograph of Grace which had been taken shortly before his wife died.

Two days ago it had disappeared from the desk in his study. Cathy claimed that she had caught Fern burning it up in the open fire when she walked in unexpectedly.

Which, the older woman pointed out, could have happened easily enough, what with Fern having the run of the house now that she came in evenings to take phone messages when Bert was out making house calls.

"More than once I've caught her burning things that belonged to Grace. Seems like she wants to rid the house of every trace of Cathy's mother."

"And what does Fern say happened to the picture?" Tracy asked, her tone both worried and guarded. The last thing she wanted was to become involved in this kind of a three-ringed dispute.

While her sympathies were all with Cathy, the fact remained that Bert Brooks was her boss. It was the letter from him which had finally persuaded her to give up her work as a psychiatric nurse and return to Oakwood.

He had been appointed, so he wrote, to head the medical staff at the new hospital, and she was his first choice to take charge of the children's section.

"You'll be doing a great service to an old friend if you decide to come," he had written; "an old friend you once promised to marry if I'd wait until you grew up. Remember? Well, I didn't wait, and you went away to make a fine record for yourself in the nursing profession. But I believe we could enjoy a fine relationship as doctor and nurse, working in harmony together, both dedicated to the fine art of healing."

It certainly had been a beautiful letter; very moving, in fact, to a girl who couldn't forget how she had once built this man up into a romantic ideal.

"It fair to burned me up," snapped Annie angrily, "the way I heard him scolding that poor motherless child this morning."

He had, Tracy gathered, accused Cathy of becoming a psychopathic liar, and threatened to send her to a place for disturbed problem children if he caught her in any more lies. Then he had ordered her to go to her room and stay there for the rest of the day.

"Like a little prisoner, Tracy, like she was being put in solitary confinement. He even

25

ordered me not to go near her. Don't you think that was unjust and cruel and just a plain awful way for a father to treat his dear little girl?"

Cathy was a dear little girl. Even allowing for the fact that the housekeeper was emotionally upset, Tracy felt herself becoming infected with Annie's righteous indignation. Knowing what she did – which no one else in this town knew – about Fern Wilson's past, she did not find it inconceivable that a perfectly honest little girl was at the mercy of a woman who was irresponsible, if not downright evil.

"But what can I do about it, Annie?"

"*You* weren't ordered not to go near the child."

So why shouldn't she just drop in for a little visit while Annie was out doing the marketing? "I'll just get out the car and scurry along uptown, while you run up and try to comfort that sweet little put-upon child."

Tracy was not enthusiastic about the idea, and by the time she was inside the house and on her way upstairs, she was sorry she had let herself be persuaded. But the minute she was inside Cathy's room, she was thankful she had come.

Cathy was a slight, fair-haired child with

26

dark eyes seemingly too big for her pale, thin face. When Tracy opened the door, she was sitting on the edge of her bed, staring into space. She had on jeans, a blue sweater, and her hair hung loose below her shoulders. "Hello," she said dully. She made an effort to smile which didn't quite come off.

"Hi, honey," Tracy said lightly, and went to the bed, where she put her arm around the girl. "No school today?"

"I'm being punished," said Cathy, and rebellion grew in the dark eyes, "for something I didn't do." Then suddenly and impulsively she flung both thin arms around her friend, and the tears came.

"Oh, Tracy, what am I to do? What am I to do?"

The tear-stained cheek strained against the arm that held her close. "I'm so alone. I want my mother so. My father don't like me any more. He hates me, and I wish I was dead."

"Now, darling, that's a silly thing to say," said Tracy, and wished she hadn't. When a heart was breaking and there was no one to give love and comfort, a child could long to be out of it all, the same as an older person.

It took her some minutes to get the story out of Cathy. It was much the same as the one Annie had told her, except for one somewhat gruesome detail. "She was dancing," blurted the child.

"What are you talking about, honey? Who was dancing?"

"That horrid Fern." Cathy seemed unable to speak of her future stepmother without coming up with an unpleasant epithet. "She *is* horrid." The dark eyes lifted, blazing with young hatred. "She hates me. And she's turning my dad against me. And she was dancing when I went in and saw her pitching Mother's picture in the flames. She was holding it up high, all the time dancing around in a little circle, like she was crazy or something."

Crazy! That word hit Tracy with the force of a small bombshell, as she thought: *Out of the mouths of babes –*

"Then she pitched the picture straight into the fire. She laughed when she did it. Then she saw me. And she came and grabbed my shoulders, real hard, like, so hard it hurt. And she said: 'You might as well keep your mouth shut about what you think you saw, you little snoop. If you don't, I'll make you wish you had.' "

Pleading eyes looked into Tracy's. "You do believe me, don't you? Oh, please believe me! If I can't make somebody believe me, I don't know what I'll do."

28

Tracy didn't know what to believe.

She needed a few minutes to think this over, and on the pretext of wanting to wash her hands, she went across the hall to the bathroom.

Scarcely aware of what she was doing, she slipped off Martha's gorgeous diamond and laid it carefully on the glass shelf below the mirror. She took soap and water to her hands. As she dried them, she stood, thinking hard.

On the face of it, Cathy's story did sound a bit fantastic. And it was wise to remember that an emotionally upset child could dream up a wild story, then convince herself that it was true. Cathy had been emotionally upset ever since she had lost her mother.

"She took it very hard, poor child," Tracy's own mother had told her that.

"Everyone felt so sorry for her. She became downright hysterical when they lowered the coffin into the grave, and afterwards she was sick in bed for weeks."

Forgetting all about her ring, Tracy went back to the bedroom, where Cathy was walking up and down, restless, shaky, unnerved, like a frightened, caged little animal.

Slipping her arms around her, Tracy thought, I can think of a dozen reasons why her story might be a lie. *But I believe her*. She said comfortingly: "I'm on your side, darling. I know you're good and honest, and if you want me to, I'll talk to your father."

Tracy had her grave doubts if that would do any good. But she could try.

"Oh, will you?" Big dark eyes lighted with a glimmer of hope. "If you could just make him believe that I'm telling the truth!" The small voice came desolate again, almost without hope. "If you could just make him love me again."

"He hasn't stopped loving you, Cathy."

"Yes, he has, ever since he fell in love with that hateful Fern."

Tracy smiled. "Let's say he's just a little mixed up, honey. Men get that way at times. And I want you to remember this. *I love you*." And, said Tracy, if things at home ever seemed more than she could take, Cathy was to call a cab and come to the old house on Elm Avenue.

"Mom and I could use a little girl in that sprawling old rattletrap. So you think of our house as your second home. Promise?"

Cathy nodded, and Tracy left, closing the door softly. When she got to the bottom of the stairs, she met Bert, who was just coming in.

"Well, hello there," he said. He had a deep, vibrant voice, a magnetic voice, according to some of his female admirers, who were

30

legion. His flashing smile was something rather special, too. Tracy was treated to the smile as he went on: "Glad you're taking the afternoon off. Lord knows you need a rest. You've earned it."

"What I need, Dr. Brooks, if for us to have a little heart-to-heart talk."

"Why all the formality?" He laughed. "You wouldn't be forgetting that we're pals of long standing, would you?" As for the little talk – "Some other time, Tracy." At the moment he was terribly rushed. He really hadn't a moment to spare.

"Please spare me the excuses," Tracy interrupted curtly. "You might spare me the bit about our being old pals, too. I don't happen to be in a palsy-walsy mood."

She might have added, but didn't, that she was in as mean and fighting a mood as she had ever experienced in her whole life. Adjuring herself silently to play it cool, she suggested pleasantly that they go around to the annex where he had his office.

Looking both puzzled and slightly annoyed, the doctor studied her for a moment. Then he smiled, nodded, and said over his shoulder, as he led the way around the garden path to the office entrance, that their talk would have to be brief.

He said that Fern was due any minute to

go over the mail with him. "She handles my correspondence and private bills, you know. Does it remarkably well, too." He added: "She's really a very remarkable girl: beautiful as a dream and smart as a whip. I've never known anyone quite like her."

How true, thought Tracy.

If there was any basis for her secret, nagging suspicions about Fern Wilson, how very, very true. He had never known anyone like her, and – with luck – never would again.

She followed him into the office with a frown on her face.

Chapter Four

As the medical man who was, and always had been, ambitious to attract wealthy patients and cash in on his work, Dr. Bert Brooks had a lot going for him.

He was, to start with, almost unbelievably handsome. With his heavy-lidded, melting dark eyes, he could charm old ladies, flat on their backs with the infirmities of age, into imagining that the sweetheart of their youth had returned to them, and with him, their own youth.

Such moments of senile dreaming never lasted, of course. But while they did last, they were really lovely, so lovely that occasionally the old ladies resolved to remember him in their wills.

Thus, very recently, the doctor had received a windfall of twenty thousand dollars. "He'd have done wonderfully well as a con man." That was the opinion of Marge Lake, an excellent nurse but a born cynic. She held to the old-fashioned idea that doctors should confine themselves to employing their medical skill. She had, said Marjorie, when holding forth at her waspish best, nothing but contempt for a medico who overworked his charm on bedridden, helpless old ladies who must soon depart this world and the fortunes left them by their long dead husbands.

As for Bert Brooks, she considered him arrogant, insufferably conceited, and inclined to look down on the nurses as inferior beings. And when a nurse dared to cross him or tell him off, she'd better watch out.

In short, the tart-voiced Marjorie took a somewhat dim view of Dr. Bert Brooks, and a few of the other girls agreed with her.

On the whole, however, the little band of women in white at Oakwood Hospital soon fell under the spell of the man's charm and good looks. They thought he was absolutely wonderful, and who was to say which group was right, which wrong?

Give the man a break. It wasn't his fault that nature had been overly kind when it endowed him with a fine, muscular physique and a profile that would have made him a fortune on the screen. As a medical student, he had made an excellent record. He did his best to keep up with all the fast and ever-increasing advances in medical research. He tried hard to be as good a doctor as he possibly could. And according to his own reasoning, it wasn't any crime for a medical man to want to make all the money he could.

Pursuing that line of thought a bit further, wealthy patients needed medical help as well as poor ones, didn't they? So if a doctor preferred the kind of patient who was able to pay his or her bills, and wouldn't gripe about a big bill, what was wrong with that?

Marjorie was dead right, however, in one of her criticisms. Neither Bert, the man, nor Bert, the head doctor at Oakwood, took gracefully to being crossed or to being told a few unpleasant truths about himself.

Everything he had ever wanted in his whole life had come his way with not too much effort on his own part. He had been popular at school. Girls had always been crazy about his spectacular good looks. He had learned

34

easily. The professors at medical school liked him. Everybody liked him, including the old ladies who remembered him in their wills. So why shouldn't he have considered himself quite a fellow?

And why shouldn't it rub him the wrong way to be informed in no uncertain terms that he wasn't the six-foot bundle of perfection which he seemed to believe he was?

That was where Tracy made her mistake that day, if you wanted to call it a mistake.

I'm glad I told him off, she assured herself when she left his office. Even at that, she hadn't said half that she was tempted to say.

Their "little talk" began pleasantly enough.

"Smoke?" asked Bert, after getting her seated in the green leather chair beside his circular, somewhat imposing desk.

He pushed a silver cigarette case across the desk, bestowed his flashing smile, thanked her for the way she had stayed on the job during the day, and into the nights, since the fire, and offered his opinion as to what had started the fire.

"I think it was a bunch of juvenile delinquents," he said.

"Do you?"

"Sure. Don't you?"

Tracy shrugged. "Who knows?"

After a moment's scowling thought, Bert

advanced the opinion that a good part of the trouble everywhere these days could be traced straight back to indulgent parents who failed to discipline their children properly.

"I," said Bert, "believe in discipline. Strict discipline," he added, to stress the point. "Make a kid understand if he doesn't do what's right, you'll crack down on him. See what I mean?"

Tracy studied him thoughtfully. "Was that the idea," she asked quietly, "behind shutting Cathy in her room today; cracking down on her for something she swears she never did?"

"I don't intend to let my child develop into a psychopathic liar. And what's more –" his face seemed to freeze as he rose – "I can't see that Cathy's behavior, or what I do about it, is any business of yours. If that's what you wanted to talk about, consider our little talk finished."

"Before it's even started?" asked Tracy, struggling to keep her tone calm and friendly.

After all, she pointed out, there were two sides to every story. "You seem to have refused to listen to Cathy's side. Do you think that's fair?"

"I," he said tightly, "have the word of the very lovely girl I plan to marry. I trust her word utterly."

"Why?"

"Why shouldn't I?"

Tracy hesitated, afraid of saying too much. "Well –" she drew a deep breath – "from what my mother has told me, Grace was a wonderfully good mother who taught Cathy to be completely honest. There was never any trouble with her until Grace was gone. Was there?"

"Let's leave Grace out of this," he said tightly.

"But how can we leave her out of it? I'm told that almost her last words were: *Love Cathy, take good care of her.*"

Ignoring the gathering fury in his face, she went doggedly on. "So now a lovely creature arrives in town with a somewhat vague but sad story about her past." Suddenly she stood up, outrage growing in her own deep blue eyes.

She stood in front of him.

"Actually, you know nothing about Fern Wilson or her background except what she has told you.

"I know everything about her!" A remark which Tracy instantly averred was utterly silly. "*No* man knows everything about *any* woman. But you do know that Fern seems to be making a practice of accusing Cathy of lying. And you accept what she says, never giving your little girl the benefit of the doubt.

How do you think Grace would feel about that, if she could know?"

With a savage glare Bert turned away from her and walked out of the office, slamming the door behind him. As she lighted a cigarette, Tracy's glance followed him. She could see him standing on the small flagstone patio outside. Oh, what's the use? she thought.

Why try to talk sense to a man who seemed under the spell of a fascinating girl?

On the patio, Bert lit a cigarette. He must pull himself together. He didn't want to quarrel with Tracy. The girl was a valuable asset in a small town hospital where R.N.s were hard to come by. In addition, she was an old friend. Why, heck, in the old days she had been like a kid sister, running in and out of their home at odd hours, tagging after him, looking up at him with adoring eyes.

"I wish you wouldn't marry that old Grace Bronson, Bert. Why don't you wait till I grow up? Then you could marry me." Imagine the kid saying a thing like that. He smiled, remembering.

No, he didn't want any trouble with Tracy. But why couldn't she have sense enough to keep her nose out of his personal affairs?

Cathy was *his* child, *his* problem.

If *he* was convinced the kid was showing tendencies that might develop into a real pathological problem, what right had Tracy Ross to question his decision?

And she had the effrontery to drag Grace's name into it!

He strode across the small flagstone space. He came back and stood again, leaning against a cement post. Scowling mightily, he lit another cigarette. He stared at the distant hills, blind to their coloring and beauty.

Had he believed in the possibility of spiritual materialization, he could have believed that Grace's sweet face with the big brown eyes, so like Cathy's eyes, was coming toward him through a thin veil.

You promised to love Cathy, to take good care of her.

Those had been almost her last words, but not quite. The last ones were: "Don't ever feel guilty, darling. It wasn't your fault that I ran after you tonight and fell. It isn't your fault that I'm going to die."

But it had been his fault!

At the dinner table that evening, they had quarreled over some trivial thing. Because Grace at the time was five months pregnant and having a hard time of it, she allowed her emotions to run out of control. Stormy words had been hurled back and forth, and Bert had gone into one of his occasional uncontrollable rages.

39

Accusing Grace of being a nagging shrew, of turning into another fool of a woman who went about town collecting gossip, then believing the lies she was told, he had slammed out of the house.

Out into the cold, icy night, following the worst blizzard ever to hit that Southern town. Into his car, off to make half a dozen or more house calls. Not until he was prescribing one half-grain of phenobarbital every four hours in the daytime for a patient, too worried over hospital bills and doctor's bills to sleep, did the surgeon at the hospital twenty miles away manage to contact him.

"I ran after you, darling. I wanted to tell you I was sorry about those awful things I said. I didn't mean them, sweetheart." Grace was talking, looking up at him out of those great dark eyes, her face already pale as death, her smile a small, heart-breaking effort.

Running after him, she had slipped on the icy pavement. The fall had brought on severe hemorrhaging, and by the time she was discovered by a neighbor and rushed to the hospital, it had been too late to save her life.

"It wasn't your fault, darling." Those were her dying words, the words that were to haunt him, because he didn't believe them. It *had* been his fault.

As a medical man, he knew that allowances

must be made for a girl well along in pregnancy. Nature played strange tricks with her chemical balance. Emotionally, she was subject to sudden, inexplicable upsets. He should have been more understanding.

He should never have shouted back at her, or rushed away, his last glance at her filled with something close to hate.

In time, the feeling of guilt more or less passed, possibly to bury itself in some deep, secret place within him; the place reserved for ugly truths a man can't endure facing about himself.

Then came the lost feeling.

Until she was gone, Bert had never realized how greatly he had depended on his wife to relieve him of the tedious, monotonous, never-ending details of living.

And there was the problem of Cathy.

Suddenly he was brought face to face with the fact that he was the father of a seven-year-old child whom he did not really know. He loved her. Of course he did. He was her dad, wasn't he? But as for knowing how to talk to her, or what to say when she came to him, shyly, with little problems – he was at a complete loss.

It might have been a little stranger who came to him, asking in her diffident voice: "Daddy, when another girl wants me to fight,

41

and I don't want to fight, what do I do?"

"Tell the brat to get lost."

He missed Grace terribly. He was lonely. Nothing held any real interest for him but his work. For some months he had no social contacts whatever. After a few casual and boring dinner dates with one or another of the town girls whom he knew, he promised himself: No more of that!

He was fully aware of his desirability both as an attractive widower and a rising young doctor. Every unmarried girl in town, along with her scheming mama, would be devising little plans to lure him into the matrimony trap. He had no intention of falling in with their schemes, or of being bothered with them.

For the first time in his entire thirty-five years, Dr. Bert Brooks was an unhappy man, a miserable man, an utterly lost man.... And then, very suddenly, the miracle came to pass.

He found himself again.

He was back in a wonderfully beautiful world.

He felt reborn.

Oh, indeed it was a miracle. It all came to pass, or rather it began, on the day when a beautiful blonde girl walked into his office at the hospital.

Her hair was the shade of gold with the sun shining on it. She had black-lashed, violet-blue eyes, a small, beautifully formed figure, and the loveliest smile.

"Are you the brilliant Dr. Brooks I've heard so much about?" she asked. And then: "My name is Fern Wilson. I'm a stranger in town. I've come to ask a great favor."

He had never believed in love at first sight.

From that day on he did believe in it.

From the moment he took her hand and met those heavenly violet eyes smiling into his, he was in love.

Chapter Five

When he went back into the office, he had calmed down. "I don't want to quarrel with you, Tracy." He was almost humble as he patted her shoulder, then sat on the edge of his desk. "If I spoke sharply, I'm sorry. I confess I'm a bit on edge these days." He picked up a medical magazine, flung it down and asked: "Do you imagine it's easy for me, saddled with the problem of a seriously disturbed nine-year-old child?"

Saddled.

Tracy frowned at the word. Fingering a cigarette which was unlit, she spoke carefully. "Cathy is a very unhappy child. She has lost the mother she loved dearly. She has adjustments to make, and no one to help her understand how to make them. She needs love terribly. I don't believe it's an exaggeration to say that she's literally starved for love. Why don't you try to understand these things?"

Her voice sharpened as she stood up. "Why don't you stop repeating rubbish somebody else has fed to you, about her being a disturbed problem kid? She isn't.

"She happens to be my child. I'd say that qualifies me to know a little more about her than you do.

"And I'd say you know nothing about her, because you haven't bothered to find out."

His smile was tight. "What do you think I've been doing these last months?"

Unable to hold the words back, she burst out: "Going slightly out of your mind over a beautiful blonde!"

There was a touch of amusement in his tone. "If I didn't know better, I'd say you were jealous."

"Would you?" Such a silly comment not being worth taking seriously, Tracy said this

44

was no time for tired little jokes. She wanted to know if he was actually planning to marry Fern Wilson in the near future.

"I am."

The look she gave him suggested that he was committing some heinous crime. "A moment ago you mentioned the word *saddled*. So you plan to saddle Cathy with a woman she intensely dislikes for a stepmother. Have you given any thought to what that will do to a sensitive, still heartbroken child?"

She took a step toward him, deep blue eyes flashing. "If she ever should develop into a serious problem case, you will have made her one, Bert Brooks – you and your Great Romance."

Still managing to hold his temper in check, Bert left the desk, walked to the window, walked back and lit another smoke.

"You have just hit close to the real problem, Tracy."

He was, he repeated, planning to marry Fern very shortly. He was not the kind of man to go on forever without a companion, a wife. Having had the good fortune to find the girl who was exactly right for him, he did not mean to let the grass grow under his feet.

"I want her and she wants me." Excitement grew in his voice. "And I don't intend to allow the rebellious antics of a jealous, psychotic child to spoil my life."

"For a medical man," Tracy retorted, "you use that word *psychotic* very loosely. You have not one shred of evidence to suggest that Cathy is schizophrenic. To say such a thing about a lost, unhappy child is – well, you should be ashamed of yourself."

Looking slightly ashamed, he said stiffly: "You'll have to make allowances for me. I'll confess I'm extremely upset. With good reason. Cathy took an unreasoning dislike to Fern from the start. Right then was when all her lying began."

"You don't believe her? You feel very *sure* she is lying?"

"Believe her! Of course I don't believe such rot. What do you take me for?"

Bert was walking the floor again. As he walked, he gave her an informative little lecture on the problem of motherless children who resented the idea of a stepmother. That, he stated flatly, was what this whole problem came down to. Cathy was in rebellion against the idea of another woman replacing her own mother. She would resort to any tale, no matter how fantastic, in her childish, neurotic determination to turn him against the girl she regarded as her mother's rival.

"Would you like to hear one of her really

wild distortions?"

Pausing in his restless pacing, he stood squarely in front of Tracy, who had walked to the door and was leaning against it.

"She said that one night Grace came to her in her dreams and warned her that she was in terrible danger, because her daddy wanted to marry a girl who would be mean and unkind to her. And she must pray awful hard that something would happen to stop him from doing this awful thing. See what I mean?"

"Mean about what?"

"About her wild prevarications. She runs to me with it, with any crazy, sometimes malicious notion that comes into her head, as if it were truth."

And, he said, slamming one palm with his fist, it had to be stopped. One way or another, Cathy had to be straightened out. He didn't like the idea of sending her away for psychiatric therapy. But if there were no other solution, he would have to do it.

"I have only her best interests at heart, Tracy, believe me. I want my child to grow up to be a responsible, well adjusted individual, a daughter I can be proud of."

"I see." Tracy took a deep breath, calculated that it would be all her job was

47

worth if she said the words in her mind, and proceeded to say them.

"Well, if you'd like a suggestion from me, Bert, why not give a little thought to yourself, as a man who is neither responsible nor well adjusted? One question." Her eyes held his. "Can you truly say that you're proud of yourself?"

Having a terrific ego, for a moment he could not take her words seriously. He laughed. "If you really want an answer, *yes*. I'd say I have a right to be proud of my record. I'm a successful medical man and –"

"And a failure as a person," she interrupted her words as sharp and cold as dripping icicles. "As a human being, as a man, you're still a spoiled, irresponsible mama's boy."

Heat growing in her voice, she rushed on. She saw his face whiten with anger.

"Your doting mother spoiled you rotten when you were a kid," she told him. Then, as he moved on into the grown up world, other women had spoiled him. Infatuated girls. Teachers who considered him brilliant and handsome. Finally Grace had taken up where the others left off.

"Grace adored the ground you walked on. She dedicated her life to helping you get ahead. In addition to running your home and bearing your child, Grace found time

48

to qualify as a laboratory technician, so she could take over your lab work. You took it all for granted. You leaned on Grace like a crutch. And that's why you were so lost when she died. Your crutch was gone."

He opened the door. "You'd better go, Tracy." The look he gave her was filled with dislike.

"So what do you do?" she went on determinedly, ignoring his suggestion that she get out. "Do you face up to the responsibility of a little daughter in the formative years? Do you accept the fact that you must be both father and mother to this child, that you must give her great love to make up for all she has lost, try to establish real communication with her?"

Her laughter was sudden, hard. "Not you. You've done exactly what any spoiled kid would do. First you had a nice, deep attack of self-pity. Why should all this happen to you? It didn't seem fair, did it?"

"Tracy, for the last time –"

"Yes?"

"You're forgetting yourself. I won't be talked to like this."

"Why not? Because it's the first time you ever looked into a mirror that wasn't flattering?" She laughed. "Now if you'll please let me finish – What you wanted was to have life beautiful again, the way it used to be. When Fern Wilson came along, she seemed like the answer to a prayer. To put it another way –" She paused to catch her breath.

"And quote a few of the town gossips, all of a sudden you seemed to lose a few of your marbles. Maybe that's why you're ready to throw poor Cathy to the wolves."

He was too furious to speak.

He caught her arm roughly, giving her a not exactly gentle shove out to the patio.

As he did so, Fern Wilson came around the path from the house. She had a mink stole slung over her shoulders, and her voice was like the tinkling of silver bells.

"Oh, dear, I hope I'm not sneaking up on a little romance with one of the nurses. Am I, darling?"

Tracy said: "Hello, Miss Wilson," and started down the path. Then she turned back.

"In case someone slips up and forgets to give you the message I left, you can check little Leah off your list of volunteer visits. You are to stay out of her room."

As she spoke, Tracy studied the violet eyes which met hers for a moment. She had done this before, searching for some sign of recognition.

Fern looked back at her puzzledly, slightly astonished. "You mean I'm not to go near that sweet little suffering child? But Leah Ormsby is one of my favorites. She's such a little darling, and my visits seem to cheer her up no end. Why must I stay away from her?"

"Dr. Sizer's order," Tracy said briefly, and glanced at Bert, whose lips had thinned angrily.

"I'm in charge of the hospital," he snapped. "I have the say as to procedures. That quack can't dictate to me."

"Quack?" Tracy's frown registered pretended surprise.

"Surely you aren't referring to Larry Sizer, with his wonderful record at that famous Western clinic."

"A blasted hypnotist," Bert's glare was downright vitriolic. "And don't give me the bit about hypnosis being used by some of the modern doctors. I have the right to my own opinion. I say a man who uses it is a quack or a charlatan or both."

"Exactly what they said in the nineteenth century," Tracy observed sweetly.

Bert actually shouted. "I won't have the quack throwing his weight around in my hospital."

"But you don't exactly own the hospital,"

51

Tracy replied gently. "And I'm very sure Dr. Sizer has every right to lay down the rules for his own patients."

"He's a fool. Why shouldn't Fern go into that child's room?"

"I can't understand it." The silver-belled voice held bewilderment. "I've tried so hard to help the poor doomed child. Why, the very last time I was with her, she had just waked up from a frightful nightmare. Something about burning in hell fires." Fern shook her golden head. "Such a time I had calming her down."

Tracy glanced at her. "A question, Miss Wilson. Many children have a tendency to play with matches. Did you, as a little girl, ever have a problem of that sort?"

Tracy was positive she saw stark fear flash in the lovely violet eyes. But like flashed lightning, it was gone in a second.

"What a question!" The tinkling voice held laughter. "Of course I liked to play with matches. What child doesn't?"

Tracy frowned thoughtfully, then turned and walked down the path to her car.

It was less than a mile to the less fashionable area of town, but the drive seemed long and wearisome. Again the headachy, feverish feeling was back. She felt awful. All she wanted was to get home and crawl into bed. Momentarily, her thoughts returned to her unpleasant session with Bert Brooks, and to the Fern Wilson problem which had been haunting her for days. But she couldn't worry any more about it just now.

She felt too ill.

Suddenly, glancing at her hand on the wheel, she was reminded that she had left the diamond ring in Cathy's bathroom. How careless of her. But the ring wouldn't walk away. I'll phone Cathy about it tomorrow, she thought, and put it out of her mind.

Chapter Six

"Tired, darling?" Fern asked as Bert led the way back into his office.

"You might call it that." He went straight to the small built-in bar and mixed two highballs. "Tracy took it upon herself to call me to task."

"About what?" asked Fern.

And when he replied: "About my handling of Cathy," she said amusedly. "The impudence of her, daring to criticize my wonderful, brilliant doctor-man."

Perching on the arm of his chair, sliding

one soft arm around his shoulders, she smiled at him. "Don't you pay her any mind, sweetheart. She's jealous."

"Jealous?"

"Of course!" Her soft laughter seemed to tremble with loving understanding. "The poor girl is madly in love with you. You told me yourself she was nuts about you when she was a kid, and she still is. Now she's so jealous she can't see straight."

"You're wrong about that, Fern." But it was food for thought.

The pretty voice had the texture of softest satin. "The trouble with you, sweetheart, is that you don't know your own enduring charm."

But to Fern it was as plain as day. Tracy's childhood infatuation with him had become a dream that refused to die. "She's never married anyone else, has she?"

"No."

"And the minute you wrote, offering her a job in the hospital, she threw up her work as a psychiatric nurse, and back she came. Didn't she?"

"Yes."

"Well, there you are!"

It was, according to Fern's caressing, faintly amused words, like the call of the siren which poor, dreaming Tracy couldn't resist.

54

Without a doubt, knowing that Bert was now a widower, her hopes were built high.

"She had her plans all made to marry you herself – the second time around." Any *woman*, said the smiling Fern, could figure that out easily enough.

"Then she arrived – and presto, her pretty, pitiful little dream was blasted to smithereens, because I had arrived and you were in love with me. So why shouldn't she go practically out of her mind with jealousy?"

Looking thoughtful, Bert agreed there might be something to that idea. Tracy was an attractive girl. He had wondered himself why she had never married. And now that he turned it over in his mind, it did seem surprising that she had accepted his hospital offer so promptly.

"So," stated Fern flatly, "she made up her mind to break us up, and she's using your little girl as her tool. She's deliberately trying to turn Cathy against me. Then she would have you believe that I'm not the right mother for the child. And the worst of it is –"

Suddenly Fern rose, frowning worriedly. "She really is exerting a bad influence over Cathy, and frankly, Bert, it's my belief you should keep her away from your daughter."

"Oh, come now, honey. Now you're the one who's imagining things," he said, pointing out that Tracy had a real gift for handling children, for winning their confidence and love. Yet he was obscurely worried as he got up, and mixed another drink which he sipped slowly, standing by the window.

"Cathy badly needs a loving friend," he said thoughtfully. And that was what Tracy was trying to give her: loving friendship.

"Bah!" Her voice curiously sharpened, Fern went to the bar and fixed another drink for herself. "And along with all this loving friendship, she's doing her bit to turn the child into a worse liar than she already is." The words were filled with rancor as she went on stormily.

"You *know* Cathy lies; you have proof of it. Yet Tracy pretends to believe every word she says. Then she berates you for being unjust to your child." The voice softened with a sigh. "I wouldn't wonder but that she tries to make you believe that *I* am the liar, not Cathy."

Silent, Bert sipped his drink while he stared at the distant ridge of mountains. For the first time the shred of a doubt had come to disturb his mind. There were times when a man didn't know what to believe.

"I'm sure you're wrong about Tracy," he said quietly. "We had unpleasant words today. It was partly my fault, I guess. She is deeply concerned about Cathy and has her best interests at heart."

"In other words, you don't believe that Tracy would twist things to suit her own purposes, or try to poison Cathy's mind against me."

He hesitated. "I'd find all that very hard to believe, Fern."

"Why?" she demanded sharply. "Plenty of girls will resort to anything, anything at all, when they're mad about a man and want to get him away from another girl. You must know that."

"Yes. Plenty of girls are like that, no doubt. But not Tracy Ross. Having known her since childhood, I know her to be basically honest, a girl with character. I'm very sure she wouldn't stoop to the kind of trickery you are trying to pin on her."

That stopped her for a moment, but it didn't kill the look of fury which flashed across the violet eyes as she walked up to him. Turning, Bert caught the fleeting expression and had the unpleasant feeling that he was looking at a stranger he had never seen before.

"You fool, you," she snapped hotly. "You sound like you were half in love with your precious Tracy. Maybe you are."

He smiled at that suggestion, then gathered her into his arms. "Silly girl," he whispered, smoothing back the golden waves that were like spun silk against his fingers. "You know whom I love. You know the girl I'm crazy about – and her name isn't Tracy."

"But you raved on and on about her beautiful character and all." Now her voice was soft and lovely as the warm, responsive body he held close to his heart.

"So I did, honey," he admitted, laughing. "But when it comes to love and marriage, I'll leave the beautiful character for some other guy." He added: "You're the girl I want, sweetheart," and excitement throbbed in his voice.

"Oh, darling," she breathed, pressing her cheek against him, "I love you so much." Her trembling arms tightened around his neck.

"I just can't wait for us to be married, darling. I'm getting so impatient."

"As I am, my precious darling."

A soft, sad sigh. "But right now everything seems so absolutely hopeless."

Slightly startled, he held her away to gaze into her eyes, which again seemed to take on the strange, hostile expression with which he was not familiar.

"Why do you say that, Fern? I thought it was all settled, that we would marry in another six weeks or so."

"Nothing is settled!" she snapped, and

withdrew completely from his arms.

Appalled, he asked what she meant, and her reply was swift. She had no intention of marrying him until some arrangement was made to dispose of Cathy.

"*Dispose* of her?" Startled, aware of very real anger, he reminded Fern that Cathy was not a pet animal – like a cat – to be gotten out of the way by a call to the Humane Society.

"She's my child and I love her," he said curtly, even though he might not be much of a hand at showing his love.

It had been an unfortunate slip of the tongue for which Fern could have bitten out her own tongue. "What an awful thing for me to say," she said contritely, and caught his hands. "But I didn't mean it the way it sounded. You know I didn't, my sweet."

What she meant was that Cathy must be sent somewhere, a school or some place, where whatever problems she had could be straightened out by experts. If a mental hospital was required, then that would be best for all concerned. Wouldn't it?

"Darling, I've tried so hard to get close to her, to make her understand that I do love her and want to take her mother's place." With a helpless shake of her head: "You must believe I've tried in every way I can think of."

But Cathy rejected every advance she made.

59

Take today, for instance, not half an hour ago, when she reached the house, she had gone in the front entrance. And when she heard Cathy sobbing – or what sounded like sobbing – she had gone upstairs to see what was wrong.

"I opened her door, and what happened?"

What happened, according to Fern, was that Cathy had advanced on her and actually slapped her face. She had told Fern to get out of her room, never under any circumstances to come in it again. "And she said – I'm quoting her very words, darling: 'If you marry my father and come here to live, I'll set fire to the house when you're asleep. Then I'll be rid of you.' Oh, Bert dear, don't you see how hopeless it all is?"

Silent, but visibly shaken, the man bit hard on his underlip.

The soft, pleading voice went on. She longed to be married to him, to belong to him in every sense. "I want to make a sweet, lovely home for you and be a wife you can be proud of. I want to set a lovely table and be a perfect hostess when your friends come. Most of all, I want to create an atmosphere of peace and comfort and love for you to come home to. But how can I possibly do all that with a problem child who hates me forever trying to create trouble between us?"

60

Then, again all soft, loving woman, she went back to his arms to whisper, as she cuddled against him: "There's only one answer. She must be sent away somewhere. Don't you see it's inevitable?"

Chapter Seven

Tracy roused out of a sound sleep, trying to push her shoulders free. Free of what? It was as if a heavy hand were bearing down on her, trying to force her to remain still.

But of course there was no hand. There was no one in the room. There was nothing.

The room was still dark. The illuminated dial on her bedside clock told her that it was only four o'clock. She shivered under the down puff her mother had put on the bed. She felt icy cold, as if she had no blood circulation at all, maybe because she had been sleeping so soundly. And maybe that was why the dream had seemed so real, because she was so deep in sleep.

Finally she got up, struggled across the room to shut the window, then went to the small gas heater to light it and get a little warmth in the room. Then she went back to bed again, huddled under the covers, arms squeezed together, closed her eyes, and thought about the dream.

In a way, she wished she could go back to sleep and recapture the dream again.

In another way, she didn't.

She was sitting in the church on that long ago afternoon when she had been twelve. The organ chords of the Lohengrin Wedding March filled the little girl's heart with sick despair. "Doesn't the bride look beautiful?" whispered her mother, beside her, as Grace Bronson, now Grace Brooks, came up the aisle on her brand-new husband's arm at the end of the marriage ceremony.

Grace had indeed looked beautiful. She was a lovely-looking girl, fair-haired, with big luminous brown eyes; a girl as good and sweet and kind as a person as she was exquisite to look at. Everyone in town said so.

The little girl, watching with bleak eyes, with unutterable misery drenching her entire being, had no reason whatever to dislike Grace, or to consider her the worst enemy she had on earth, or to make up her mind, then and there, that she would ruin Bert Brooks' life.

None, that is, except that she was in love with the handsome, tall, dark-eyed groom herself.

Said Tracy to her mother that evening as she nibbled at tasteless food: "She'll ruin poor Bert's life. I just know she will."

Her mother said amusedly: "Tracy, honey, you mustn't take this wedding so to heart. Do try to drink your milk, dear. It's good for you. Just because Bert has been like a big brother to you, you mustn't resent his marriage to Grace. She's a lovely girl."

"I suppose she is," Tracy conceded, "in a way. But she isn't the right wife for him. She isn't suited to him."

"What makes you say that?"

"Well, Bert is such a *special* person. You know he is, Mother." And Grace was – well, the only word the little girl could think of was *ordinary*. "She isn't in the least brainy." And as for her looks – "Of course, right now she's sort of pretty. But she's the type who will fade very fast."

Sally had chuckled. She could recall, she said, being madly in love with her Sunday School teacher when she was around ten. He was a man old enough to be her father. "He had a wife, a stout, friendly, pleasant middle-aged woman – and oh, how I hated her!" But, said Sally: "I got over it, and so will you."

Falling in love with an older man, explained Tracy's mother, was much like measles. Many little girls suffered an attack of it. But after it went away, they could scarcely remember what it was like.

However, Tracy remembered.

She had remembered in the dream from which she had just awakened. In the course of the dream, flashes of that awful day had come back to her. Her inner ear had heard the echo of organ music, and the echo of her own intense words: *"She'll ruin his life."*

The pale light of early dawn began to sift into the room. She sat up, pushing back her hair. The shivery feeling was gone. Now she felt hot, feverish. Her mother had left a glass of orange juice on the bedside table. She took a sip of it and said softly, aloud: "Could it possibly be that I've never gotten over it?"

Could that be one of the reasons she felt such an intense dislike of Fern Wilson?

Don't be ridiculous, she scoffed silently, conducting an inner dialogue with herself. You dislike her because you know some very unpleasant things about her. Because of this, you suspect every move she makes. And why shouldn't you?

Yes, I know. But under the circumstances, I should give her the benefit of the doubt. Even if some of my suspicions are justified, I should feel sorry for her. Shouldn't I?

Oh, sure. But feeling sorry for her was one

64

thing. Watching her captivate Bert Brooks and scheme to push his daughter out into the cold was quite another.

Bert Brooks. Bert Brooks. It always got back to him, didn't it? So why not face any ghosts that might be lurking in the closet of her deeply buried childhood fantasies?

Why don't you forget your suspicions of Fern Wilson for a few minutes? Turn your little searchlight on yourself for a change. Ask yourself a few questions about yourself.

Such as?

Ha. As if you didn't know. Well, for a starter, how come you've never married? Lord knows, it isn't because you haven't had chances.

Right.

Tracy was a girl whom men found extremely attractive.

Without working at it, she could think of several proposals of marriage that had come her way in the last few years. Two had been from young, ambitious, quite attractive young doctors. And there had been a certain patient – a successful and wealthy businessman.

He had promised her: "If the docs get me through this heart attack, I'll take you any place in the world you'd like to go. Rome, Naples, Paris, anywhere. You name it, and we'll go there." And if he didn't survive, she would inherit his entire fortune.

Tracy smiled at him, told him he was a darling. She was sure he would get well, and she liked him very much. But love him she did not. And since, in her book, marriage must include very deep and real love, she was sorry but – no, thanks.

Her answer had always been no, because she seemed unable to respond to any man with love. Now why was that?

She had asked herself the question a thousand times over. She still didn't know the answer.

And here's another question. How did it happen you threw up your psychiatric nursing at the drop of a hat? Or, to put it more exactly, the very day she read Bert Brooks' letter, offering her the job in Oakwood?

Oh, well, there were several sound answers to explain that decision.

For one thing, as a psychiatric nurse, she had just about had it. The work was not only hard work; it was also rough work.

Handling violent cases demanded something in addition to nurse's training. It needed the kind of strong, husky, muscular body which she didn't have.

Then, too, following her dad's death a year ago, her mother had been left completely alone. In many of Sally's letters, there had been hints of her terrible loneliness, of how awful it was to have no one to love or do for. She wrote once: "Loneliness follows me like a shadow."

And then she had written: "Oh, Tracy, if only I could have *you* with me. But I know your work makes this impossible."

However, after Bert's hospital offer, it was no longer impossible. Telling herself that her mother was her main reason for coming back, she had decided almost instantly to come.

But had she been lying to herself?

What about her knowledge that Bert Brooks was now a widower with a young daughter who would need a mother, and with a fairly pretentious home that would have a crying need for a woman's knowing hand?

What about the fairly obvious fact that, for a variety of reasons, Bert would marry again, sooner or later?

Yeah. What about all that? whispered that tiny inner voice. Are you very, very sure you were thinking primarily of your mother when you made up your mind to come back?

She was no longer sure of anything, except that her temperature had shot up and she was probably going to be really ill.

Chapter Eight

Tracy again fell into a troubled sleep, and awakened to bright sunshine. Her mother, a small, brisk woman with fluffy white hair, did not bother to conceal her anxiety. "You been moaning and groaning, honey," she said, standing by the bed with worried eyes. "And you need a fresh gown. This one is soaked through."

She went to the closet. "Try to sit up, dear. I'll help you change." Returning to the bed with a sheer white gown and Tracy's padded blue robe, she wanted to know how her girl felt.

"Not too good." Having never before felt so weak and shaky, Tracy realized she would never make it to the hospital. She made no protest when Sally said emphatically that she needed a doctor.

But when she started from the room, saying she would phone Bert Brooks right away, Tracy replied with a firm *no*.

"Call Dr. Sizer, Mother."

Her mother turned, staring at her with surprised eyes. "Larry Sizer? But, honey, people say that man hypnotizes his patients!

What you've got is a heavy cold and most likely one of those virus infections. What in heaven's name do you want with a hypnotist?"

Tracy smiled back at Sally with faint amusement. "He's an excellent physician, Mother. Because he uses hypnotism very occasionally with special cases, people, who don't understand what it's about, refer to him as a hypnotist."

Thus, said Tracy a bit tartly, they displayed their ignorance. She added: "He's the man I want to come, Mother."

Larry came in less than an hour. When he walked into the room, Tracy said hello, then informed him that her temperature was way up and still climbing. No doubt her blood pressure was way down. During the night she had had a bad nightmare and a bad chill, followed by a drenching sweat. In short, she was a mess.

"Now that we have all that cleared up, Dr. Sizer –" If he would draw up a chair, she would explain what he could do for her.

Grinning, he dragged a chair from across the room, suggested that she call him Larry and let him get a word in edgewise. There was amusement in his voice.

"It's customary for the doctor to ask the questions, young lady, then make the decisions." In addition, it was simply

69

common courtesy, professional courtesy so to speak, to permit the doctor to show off his bedside manner.

"Pooh!" scoffed Tracy with a sudden grin. "You never bother with the bedside manner bit. You know you don't. And as for answering the questions before you ask them, I'm simply trying to save time."

He studied her thoughtfully. "Would you care to explain why you sent for me?" She should stay in bed, drink hot liquids, take aspirin. Obviously she didn't need to be told this would be the best advice he could give her. So why?

She hesitated, meeting his eyes squarely before she said: "I have to get that monkey off my back. You know? The one you mentioned yesterday."

Suddenly her voice grew ragged. "I am worried sick. It may well be the reason I'm stuck here in bed with fever and the shakes."

He touched her hand gently, something like compassion in his eyes studying her gravely.

"In short, something is bugging you, and you need to talk it over with someone."

"Yes."

"So you picked me for your listening ear."

She nodded. "You told me I could."

"Yes. So I did."

"I've thought and thought. And there isn't

anyone else in this town I can talk to."
Because, she added, there wasn't anyone else
she could trust to keep her confidence or have
the wisdom to advise her.

"But you do trust me," he said gently,
thoughtfully. "Why?" he asked, after a
moment's silence.

Their eyes met, and Tracy had the curious
sensation that something like a powerful
electric current passed between them. "I don't
know why I trust you." The words were little
more than a murmur. "I just do."

She tore her eyes away from his and thought
for a moment. Her next words were brisk,
almost peremptory. "I want you to get me
back on my feet as soon as possible, say by
tomorrow. Can you do that?"

"I can't hurry nature, Tracy. I'd say several
days in bed would do you a lot of good.
What's the hurry?"

Her voice was impatient. "I've got to get
something off my mind. That's why the
hurry. I must talk with you alone, strictly
alone. I must come to your office. And as for
being stuck here in bed for days –"

She made a grimace. "I'd simply think and
think, worry and worry." By the end of a
week there was a good chance she'd be a
raving maniac.

She said a bit wildly: "If you can't get me

back on my feet any other way, hypnotize me
– and order me to get up."

He threw back his head and laughed.
Then, informing her that he was not a
stage magician, he agreed to give her some
potent vitamin shots. He promised no miracle,
but he would promise to come and drive her to
his office the following evening, provided, of
course, that she felt up to it.

"I'll feel up to it!" She gave him a sudden,
impish smile. "And if I don't, you can carry
me. Okay?"

"Okay." The oddly warm smile which
curved his wide mouth touched his eyes.
Nothing would give him more pleasure than
to carry a lovely blue-eyed patient from bed to
office.

He stood up, his gray eyes intent as he
stared down at her. "They are very beautiful,
you know."

"What are you talking about?"

"Your eyes, Tracy." He shook his head
suggesting the possibility that she had done a
little hypnotizing job on *him*. "When you look
at me, as you're doing now, I'd promise to do
almost anything you asked."

"Then get me up off this bed!" Her voice
was cool, almost curt. Inside, she was aware
of a strange warmth and excitement.

By the following day she actually did feel

remarkably better. She was up before noon, and spent the afternoon watching TV and fussing with her nails and hair. When Lary arrived that evening she *looked* remarkably better.

"Well," observed Larry, his first glance taking in her dress, the exact shade of her blue eyes; the white coat, soft and woolly, slung over her shoulders, "I've sometimes wished I could think of myself as a miracle worker. Looking at you, I wonder if maybe I am one."

"Let's get going," Tracy said briefly, asking as she followed him out to his car: "Before we get to your office and go into the confessional, do you promise to keep everything I tell you strictly between you and me?"

"Of course," he said.

Twenty minutes later he repeated the promise when they were seated in his office, which was a small suite adjoining the living quarters of the recently modernized house where he lived with an aunt.

As he turned on soft lights, got Tracy settled in an easy chair and brought her coffee laced with brandy, he offered a brief sketch of his living arrangements.

Aunt Carrie, he said, kept house for him, did the marketing and cooking, took phone messages, and did her utmost to find a wife for him. "You'll meet her in due course. I might as well warn you –" his grin brought a curiously boyish expression to his usually grave face – "she'll start right in trying to cook up a romance between us."

What was more, he continued, drawing up a leather chair to face her, "Aunt Carrie, although the salt of the earth, is a compulsive talker." He took a sip of coffee, then set the cup aside on his desk. "If you don't interrupt, in twenty minutes flat you'll have our family history, know what a wonder boy I always have been and how my life was once blighted by love for the wrong woman."

"I can't wait to meet her!" said Tracy. Then: "By the way, was it?"

"Was what?"

"Your life blighted by some girl?"

"Ask Aunt Carrie!"

He grinned. Then his face grew grave as he leaned toward her and took her hands, which were cold and not too steady. "All right, Tracy. Let's have it. What's the problem that seems to be haunting you like the hounds of hell?"

She stared back at him for a moment, took a deep breath, then blurted out the words: "Larry, I know something about Fern Wilson and her past that no one else in this town knows. She was once a mental patient."

His eyes registered surprise. "You're certain?"

"Oh, yes, I'm certain."

Fern had been a patient in the mental hospital where Tracy had worked for over two years. For two or three months she had been confined in the violent ward.

"Do you know what the cold pack is, Larry?"

He nodded. Yes, he knew. An ice pack under the patient's neck. Sheets wrapping the patient like a mummy. Canvas strips tight across the body at the chest, stomach, and knees. "You worked in one of those wards?"

Not for long, she said. For the most part, her work had been with less advanced cases, supervising occupational therapy. But one night, when she had been at the hospital less than a month, there was a shortage of both nurses and guards. And there was a girl who had gone dangerously berserk. First she had hurled herself against a wall, pounding the wall, then gouging at herself with the jagged top of a tin can. When she made a vicious attack on the nurse who tried to restrain her, kicking and beating at the nurse, then biting her, she was hustled upstairs to the violent ward.

"I was sent up to help fasten her into the

75

cold pack," said Tracy. After the job was done, she added, she was sick as a dog. It had been her first experience seeing the deep, dark horror of mental unbalance at its worst.

She shook her head slowly. Why she hadn't thrown up her work in psychiatric nursing the next day, she would never know. "Anyway, that was my first glimpse of Fern Wilson."

"And you've told no one?"

She shook her head. "No one, Larry."

"Don't you think you should?"

"That's my problem."

Chapter Nine

Looking thoughtful, Larry got up, hunted for his pipe, resettled himself in the big leather chair and smoked in silence for some moments before he said: "Suppose you give me a few more details. I take it she was dismissed from the hospital as cured?"

"Oh, yes. Definitely."

For some months Fern had been under the care of a psychiatrist, a woman with an international reputation, one of the best. She had been analyzed, given shock treatment, plus the usual drugs – metrazol, amatyl, and so on. There were plenty of cases where nothing worked. With Fern Wilson, something had worked, or maybe all of it together. Anyway, it was the consensus of opinion among the doctors and nurses that the woman psychiatrist had worked another of her miracles.

"It's a large hospital," Tracy explained, and she had had no further direct contact with Fern after that one awful night. But she had seen her around. After her recovery was under way and Fern was permitted to move freely around the hospital grounds, Tracy had noticed her several times. "It was hard to believe my own eyes." Once Fern began to take an interest in her hair and personal appearance, she didn't look like the same person.

"But you recognized her immediately here in Oakwood?"

Tracy nodded, recalling her startled shock that day in Campbell's drug store. It was her third day back in town. She had gone into Campbell's to get some aspirin tablets for her mother. While she was waiting to be served, her glance strayed to the soda fountain counter. There she saw her, wearing white satin pants and a green satin blouse, flashing her toothy smile at the counter boy who brought her Coke.

"Did she recognize you?" Larry asked abruptly.

"I don't think so," Tracy said, but the worried look crept into her eyes.

Many times she had wondered whether Fern could possibly have remembered the face of the nurse who had helped fasten her into that cruel but necessary canvas trap on the night when she turned into a wild thing, completely out of control.

If she did, she had given no sign.

Just to make sure it was not a case of mistaken identity, Tracy said, she had checked that same day with Celia Kelly.

The name brought a faint grin to Larry's lips. "The gal who runs the beauty parlor and keeps her customers up to date on the town gossip."

"Correct. But how did you know?"

"Aunt Carrie." His grin widened, then vanished. "Don't tell me our local Walter Winchell was nursing any suspicions as to Fern Wilson's past."

Heavens, no. But she knew all about her present, including the fact that she had arrived in town with a sad story about her dear daddy's recent death. And that she had come to this obscure Southern town to escape the sorrowful memories which New York held for her. And that she had taken an expensive apartment where she was said to be writing a book – or maybe it was a play. It might even be poetry she was dreaming up. On this point Celia was a bit vague.

But as to the sudden flaming romance between the lovely blonde girl and Dr. Bert Brooks – she was not vague. "Imagine!" marveled Celia. "Every unattached girl in this town has been after the doc, ever since his poor wife had that sad accident and left him forever. Then along comes this Fern Wilson and hits the jackpot." Oh, well, it simply went to prove what could be done with a lot of yellow hair and a baby-doll face.

Larry pondered. "Didn't it occur to you to go to Bert Brooks with the story? Didn't you feel you knew him well enough to take him into your confidence?"

Plainly this question struck Tracy as slightly ridiculous.

She laughed. "When I was a kid, I knew Bert as well as if he were my brother." Her brief smile was touched with irony. "At the ripe old age of twelve, I imagined I was madly in love with him. When he married the girl he did marry, I was absolutely positive my life was ruined. Incidentally, I was equally sure that his life would be ruined, too, because he had married the wrong girl."

"I see." Larry thought that over for quite

a while before he observed: "So now you're pretty sure his life will be ruined again – by marrying another wrong girl."

Because the words made her squirm inwardly, Tracy's retort was clipped, edged with defensive anger. "If you're implying that I'm in love with Bert Brooks *now*, you're being ridiculous." A perfectly honest answer, she was sure, since it was the conclusion that she had reached when she put the same question to herself.

"I don't agree, Tracy." It was altogether possible, he suggested, that she was still emotionally involved with the object of her childhood infatuation without realizing it. Sometimes these deeply buried emotions could carry over into later years.

"In your case, Tracy, it could explain why you're so hopelessly mixed up about this problem."

"That isn't fair!" she burst out. It didn't even make sense, because if she were jealous of Fern Wilson – "That's what you are implying, isn't it?"

"In a sense, yes."

Then why wouldn't she have rushed straight to Bert Brooks with her story? "Why don't I tell him, as I'm telling you, that his love is an ex-mental patient?"

"Because you aren't sure he'd believe you."

80

His smile was slow. "Moreover, there may be a conflict going on inside you emotionally which you don't understand."

She breathed hard, then jumped up to get the coffee urn on the electric plate. Refilling her cup, she stood in front of him. Her eyes came alive with anger and hurt. She had come to him for understanding; not to be told that emotionally she had never grown up.

"You're perfectly right," she said coldly, "about my inner conflict."

Just because she did not like Fern Wilson as a person, was that any justification for broadcasting the truth about her? Fern had been dismissed as cured. Tracy had no proof that it wasn't true, and if it were true – if she was simply a girl who sought a town where she wasn't known to escape the stigma of having once been a mental patient –

"What right have I to point an accusing finger at her? What do you take me for?" she demanded fiercely. "A witch hunter?"

He was silent, thoughtful.

And there was another angle, she reminded him. As a nurse, what might it do to her professional standing if she went about uncovering the secrets of patients in the hospital where she had once worked?

"You might lose your R.N. rating," Larry agreed, "if Bert Brooks wanted to make

81

trouble for you."

"All right, then. You must see that it isn't as simple as you're trying to make it sound."

"I didn't say it was simple," Larry contradicted. "On the contrary, it's a perplexing situation, and an ugly one. But frankly, Tracy, I don't see that it's *your* problem. Bert Brooks is a big boy. If he chooses to marry a blonde, vapid-faced girl without knowing what he's doing, that's his problem."

As for Fern Wilson, Larry admitted frankly that he couldn't stand her. He believed that she did a great deal of harm with her volunteer do-gooding at the hospital.

For the first time fierce resentment found its way into his voice. "I happen to love kids." He talked for a moment about the vivid imagination of a child, how that imagination could swiftly build some sadistic fairy tale, so called, into terrifying reality.

That, he assumed, was what happened with little Leah Ormsby. Horror stories seemed to be Fern Wilson's stock in trade. In his opinion, she was a first class idiot who had no business coping with critically ill children.

All this Larry admitted. And if, as Tracy said, the gal had a history as a violent psycho, it was something to think about.

"But I can't see why you should batter your

brains worrying about it. Look, Tracy, why don't you just put it out of your mind? Forget it. That's my advice."

"Forget it! Just like that." She leaned forward. "That's very easy to say, Larry. In fact, it was what I had been telling myself to do – until I realized what was happening with Bert's little girl."

"So we're back to Bert Brooks again." He smiled wryly.

Tracy compressed her lips, showing irritation.

"I apologize," he said quickly, taking her hand in both of his. "Look, my girl, I'm not trying to rib you or question your motives. Obviously you are taking this whole thing very much to heart." Again the crooked smile. "Every two or three sentences, and there we are – back to your twelve-year-old hero again."

Silent, she met his eyes.

Finally she told him: "Probably I shouldn't blame you for leaping to the obvious conclusion. Only you're all wrong in what you're thinking."

Still smiling, looking not at all convinced, he said pleasantly: "All right; what about the doctor's little girl? What's *her* problem?"

It didn't take very long to tell him.

"Now she's being accused of psychopathic lying."

"Accused by whom?"

"You guess." Her smile was grim. "By Fern Wilson, naturally. She's doing a really marvelous selling job on gullible, infatuated Bert – and this helpless child is the victim. She has Bert practically convinced that his little girl has developed into a psychopathic liar and should be sent somewhere for psychiatric therapy. Surely you can't deny that someone should do something about *that*."

He looked dubious. "Maybe the kid has been telling lies. Children who feel rejected sometimes do. They fib, snitch things that don't belong to them, develop temper tantrums. It's their way of attracting attention. You're a nurse with psychiatric training, Tracy. You must realize this is a distinct possibility."

"Oh, sure," she said, with a long, deep sigh. It was, she thought, much like trying to hold a conversation with a man who insisted on playing deaf, dumb, and blind. In a way, it seemed hopeless to go on talking. Still, she had to try. There was no one else to turn to.

"I know all the quick and easy answers as well as you do Larry."

But she also knew little Cathy, who had come to love Tracy as her dearest and most trusted friend. "You'll just have to take my word for it, Larry. The child is *not* a liar. It's a plain and simple case of a designing woman trying to pin wrong-doing on a child in order to get rid of her."

"Why go to all the bother?" Larry looked honestly puzzled.

With another deep sigh, Tracy wondered if the man could possibly be as dumb as he was pretending. "Could it possibly be," she inquired pleasantly, "that you've never heard of lovely, self-centered women who don't want to be bothered with a step-child when they marry Papa?"

"What about sending her away to boarding school?"

"Why ask me?" She asked for a cigarette, then pouted when Larry said smoking wouldn't do her chest condition one bit of good. "But it would do my nerves plenty of good."

"Am I getting on your nerves?" Grinning, he gave in about the cigarette and lit one for her.

"You are, definitely. Frankly, I suspect you're deliberately asking me foolish questions. I think you understand perfectly well what I'm getting at. An ex-mental case who may or may not be permanently cured has a nice child at her mercy. No matter what guilt she tries to pin on Cathy, Bert Brooks believes her. His own child he will not believe."

"Have you tried talking with him about it?"

"I have."

"And?"

"I got exactly nowhere. Correction," with a small, harsh laugh. "I was ordered out of his office."

"Because you tried to tell him the truth about Fern?"

"Good heavens, no. I just tried to tell him a few plain truths about himself. Oh, Larry, it's worrying about that child that sent me to bed ill. I'm sure it was that, mostly. I've simply got to help her somehow, some way. I'll never be at peace with myself if I don't. And, Larry –"

"Yes?"

"I've been thinking hard, and – well, I think there's a way you could help. You say you're fond of children. Believe me, you'll never find a nicer child than Cathy, or one in worse need of a helping hand. You wouldn't want to see this nice, sweet little girl railroaded into a loony-bin, would you?"

"Naturally not." But his eyes looked wary.

"You don't need me to tell you what that might do to a sensitive child. She might become really and truly deranged, from the shock of it. You're a man with a heart, Larry. I don't know you very well, but I'm very sure I'm right when I say you have compassion for the helpless, the suffering. That's true, isn't it?"

"My little inner voice whispers that you have a scheme in mind." A smile twitched his mouth. "Okay. Out with it, Tracy. And I'd take it kindly if you'd stop giving me the works with those blue eyes. When you look at me like that, I lose all reasoning power."

She gave him the sweetest of smiles. "You don't need to reason about what I have in mind. Larry, if we can get Bert's consent, would you consent to hypnotize Cathy?"

"*What?*"

"Hypnotize Cathy. If Bert heard the truth from her when she was in a hypnotic trance, then he would have to believe her. Will you?"

"No! Of all the crack-brained ideas."

"*Please.*"

Chapter Ten

Before Larry could utter another vigorous refusal, the phone rang. He went into the adjoining room to take the call. While he was gone, Tracy heard a car stop outside. Within seconds, in came a tall, thin, redheaded woman with a deep, husky voice, a radiant smile, and the announcement she was Aunt Carrie.

"Hello," Tracy said pleasantly. "I've heard about you."

"And I've heard about you, Tracy Ross." Aunt Carrie drew up a chair, declared that she had been absolutely dying to meet the nurse with the fantastic blue eyes, and she was absolutely thrilled to know that Larry had finally gotten over that selfish, greedy, impossible creature he had once been in love with.

Sheer curiosity forced Tracy to ask. *"She* wasn't in love?"

"Dear me, yes. But what she was in love with, my dear, was all the money she expected Larry to make catering to fashionable, wealthy patients. When she discovered that he had no interest in becoming a moneygrubber, she left him flat – and darling Larry went into the doldrums."

Aunt Carrie fitted a cigarette into a long ivory holder, explaining that she had quit smoking any number of times, but never for longer than three days. Honestly, for a time she had been afraid Larry was *never* going to get over that girl.

But all's well that ends well! "And now that he's met you –" Her wink and knowing little smile suggested that already she considered Tracy practically one of the family.

It was very embarrassing. Tracy said quickly: "There's nothing personal between your nephew and me, truly. I'm here tonight as a patient; nothing more."

Exactly the way Aunt Carrie had started her romance with her dear, beloved, lately departed Ben! "My husband was a doctor, too, my dear. If I hadn't stepped on a needle, we might never have met." But Carrie felt that fate arranged such little matters. To the day she died, she would believe that fate had arranged for her to ram that needle into the bottom of her foot. So off she went to Dr. Ben's office – and the next thing you knew they were married.

With a deep sigh she continued sadly: "Now my darling has passed on." But, more brightly: "We had twenty wonderful, blissful years together, so I have my beautiful memories."

In addition, she had her home in this darling little Southern town. Ben had bought it on their last long motor trip together.

"He was quite taken with Oakwood, and we agreed it would be a perfect place to come when he retired." But before he got around to retiring, he was gone. "So I talked dear Larry into coming here to live with me."

The darling boy had always thought he'd like to set up practice in a small town, and *she* thought it would be the ideal place for him to start a new life and forget *that girl*.

"So here we are," observed Aunt Carrie with her radiant smile. "And here you are!" And if that wasn't fate, she didn't know what you'd call it.

Aunt Carrie's conversation was strictly a one-way operation. She waited for no reply, and Tracy sat listening, more and more embarrassed, and thankful when Larry reappeared.

He grinned affectionately at his aunt, then reminded her that it was time for her favorite news broadcast.

"Yes, I'm going," she said, getting up. "Larry thinks I talk too much," she informed Tracy. "And of course he's right. But I do so *love* to talk. Now that my dear Ben has passed on, talking is one of the few pleasures I have left."

On her way to the door, she turned back to say: "By the way, at the club meeting tonight I heard some very sad news." Old Mrs. Renard had passed away last night in her sleep.

All the ladies had been speculating, said Carrie, as to what would happen to Martha Renard's diamonds.

After her first shock of sadness, Tracy thought, *What has happened to my diamond?*

These last two days she had felt too ill to phone and ask Cathy about the ring. Oh, well, she decided, nothing could have happened to it. She would phone in the morning.

Then, for a moment, her thoughts turned again to the old lady whom she had dearly loved. Tears filled her eyes, but they went away, to be replaced by a flash of fierce bitterness, when Larry said gently: "It's time I was taking you home, Tracy. You've worked yourself into a highly emotional state over a situation you can do nothing about."

She stood up. "I've just lost one of the dearest friends I ever had," said Tracy through gritted teeth. "Except for my mother, possibly my only friend. That's the reason I was crying."

"I'm sorry." He came to her, taking her

hand gently. "I didn't realize you and the old lady were so close. But after all –"

"After all, what?" she interrupted sharply. "And if you give me the bit about how she was old and it was time for her to go, I'll scream. I'm not crying for *her*, but for *myself*. I've lost my friend. And the way I feel right now," she rushed on, fighting the sobs which were coming in real earnest, "I have no one else I can turn to when I need help."

"You have me, Tracy."

"You!" Her laugh was scornful; she pulled her hand free. At the far side of the room there was a leather couch. Throwing herself on it, she ordered herself silently to calm down. Maybe she was cracking up, behaving like a disorganized child. But the words kept coming in a torrent.

"I ask you for help, I ask you to do one little thing for me, and what do I get? Ask for bread, and get a stone. That's the kind of help you are."

He sat beside her, pulling her upright and holding her so with a gentle arm. "Listen, my dear girl, I've given you what I believe is sound advice. If you're sore because I won't go along with the notion of trying hypnosis on the little girl, I'm sorry. But if you were thinking straight, you'd realize that it's impossible."

"Why is it impossible?"

Tracy considered it a very sensible idea.

He did not use hypnosis as a parlor trick, he told her. That was what her scheme sounded like. It had its legitimate value in certain types of therapy. Occasionally he used it in surgery, in cases where an anesthetic might mean death to the patient. It was also valuable with psychosomatic problems, such as ulcers, where he needed to get at the basic cause of the illness.

"I do not use it," he said grimly, "to find out if some little girl is telling lies." And, he added, his tone vaguely angry, she had no right to ask him to do it. "In effect," his words were clipped, "you are asking me to prostitute my work in order to prove to Bert Brooks that his girl friend isn't to be trusted. It won't work."

She was coldly furious. "So that's what you think of me! That I'm in love with Bert, trying to use you to get rid of my rival! That's what you mean, isn't it?"

His eyes were grave.

"Not exactly," he said, choosing his words thoughtfully. "Let me put it this way, Tracy. Once there was a twelve-year-old girl, a very serious-minded child, who developed an obsession about an older man."

"Me, in other words."

"Exactly. You. Well, you've grown up since then. But I'm not sure you've ever really kicked that little-girl obsession. The years have passed, but I suspect the emotional involvement with your dream man lingers on."

"That's utterly ridiculous, Larry!" But was it? Hadn't she put the same question to herself several times during these last few days? But he had no right to read her secret thoughts. It wasn't true, anyway.

She jerked free of his restraining arm and said with all the cool dignity at her command: "This has been a most interesting evening, Dr. Sizer. I thought I had found a good friend who would give me some much needed advice. I was wrong about that." She stood up before telling him tightly: "The advice I've gotten from you I could put in a thimble. But I have found out exactly what you think of me, and that's a good thing to know."

She got her coat and swung it around her shoulders before she turned to tell him: "You take me for just another idiot-girl who is mad for a man she can't get." She was breathing hard, struggling to hold back the nervous tears. "You despise me, don't you?"

He came close to her then, his eyes tender and filled with a great warmth as his arms reached and drew her close.

94

"You're talking nonsense, and I'm sure you know it." The arms drew her still closer, and she seemed powerless to resist their insistent pressure. Again her entire being seemed flooded with warmth, with a strange excitement.

"I hate you," she whispered.

"No you don't." He laughed softly, his gaze on her lifted face. "You don't hate me any more than I despise you. Don't you understand that I'm jealous of your childhood dream man?"

"You don't expect me to believe that!"

"It's hard for me to believe it myself." He smiled into her eyes. "But this I do know. You're the first girl who has interested me in many a long day. In fact, never again did I expect to find a girl I'd give a second thought to. But I've been thinking about you off and on for the last few days. I looked forward to tonight more than you'd believe. It seemed to me that something very wonderful was about to happen to me."

He broke off, his eyes suddenly flashing with anger. "And then you sit here for two solid hours talking about your worries – and they always come back to Bert Brooks. If I had a tape recording, you'd hear yourself mentioning his name about a thousand times."

"I did not."

"You did. Everything you say goes back to that guy. Why shouldn't I conclude that he's an obsession with you? Why shouldn't I be jealous?"

She broke in weakly. "I think you'd better take me home, Larry."

"I think so, too. But before we go, I want you to get one thing straight. *This* is the way I feel about you."

Swiftly she was enclosed in his arms, and his hard, demanding kiss on her lips was like no other kiss she had ever known. Before she slept that night she thought, *I'll remember it forever.*

Chapter Eleven

That same Saturday morning, around ten o'clock, Cathy Brooks was on her knees beside her bed, praying.

Just as she finished, Cathy heard the door open, and when she opened her eyes and stood up she saw Fern Wilson walking in. Fern was smiling, all ready with a cheery good morning. "Been saying your prayers, sweetie?"

When she was being mean and threatening, Cathy considered this woman, whom she thought of as her enemy, bad enough. When she put on the sugary-sweet mask, she was even more detestable. Cathy had the sure sense of a child for hypocrisy.

As Fern advanced toward her, all smiles and sweetness, Cathy's quick, angry words were definitely not those of a meek, prayerful little girl who loved her enemy.

"Miss Wilson, I've asked you never to come into my room without knocking, and asking my permission to come in."

Fern's quick laugh had a pretty silver-bells quality.

"Now, honey, what way is that for a little girl to talk, especially to someone who will soon be her mother?"

"You'll never be my mother!"

"But, darling –"

"And this room is *mine*. My mother said it was mine when she fixed it for me." Helpless tears flooded Cathy's eyes as her glance went to the drapes Grace had sewn by hand, to the pale blue padded bedspread matching the shade of the drapes. Even the dressing table and chairs Grace had enameled a pale ivory trimmed with blue. And when it was all finished, she had told Cathy: "This is your own little sanctuary, honey. Even I will never come in unless you invite me in." Grace had believed that privacy was one of the inalienable rights of a child.

"Even my own dear mother wouldn't have marched in here the way you just did. So what makes you think you have the right to do it?"

Continuing to smile, Fern sat down on the bed, crossed her legs, which were encased in black velvet pants, lit a cigarette, dropped a few ashes on the soft blue rug, and said sweetly to the angry child that she had come to smoke the pipe of peace.

"What does that mean?"

It meant, explained Fern, that she wanted them to be friends. "Let's start over, Cathy honey. I'm only too eager to love you. I want to take you to my heart as a dear, darling daughter. Can't you love me a little in return?"

"No," said Cathy flatly.

With a sigh, Fern shook her head. "Darling, you make things so difficult for me."

"Please don't call me *darling*, Miss Wilson," said Cathy curtly, and turned to see her father standing in the doorway.

"My two girls having a gab fest?" asked Bert.

"Dad –" Cathy began.

Fern broke in, her voice faintly unhappy.

98

"Bert, what am I to do about this child of yours? As I told you, I have things all planned to take her shopping. Then I thought we'd go to Henderson's for lunch, then to a show. But Cathy hasn't given me a chance to tell her about my lovely plans."

With a deep sigh: "Cathy fights me so. And it makes me so terribly unhappy. Can't you make her understand, darling, how much I truly want us to be friends?"

Bert smiled tenderly at her, his heart in his eyes. Then he looked at his daughter, who was staring at him unblinkingly, her big dark eyes so vividly like her mother's that for a moment Bert had the faintly eerie feeling that it was actually Grace looking at him.

It was hard for him to meet those eyes, which seemed alive with anguish, and he began walking back and forth across the room as he struggled to decide how to handle the situation.

"Look, Cathy," he said finally. "It will please me if you'll get that chip off your shoulder. When someone makes friendly overtures, you should meet her halfway. Right?"

"It isn't right for her, or anyone else, to come barging into my room when I don't want them in here. My own mother told me that, and I guess she knew what was right and what wasn't."

Fighting against helpless tears, she jerked away from the friendly arm Bert attempted to put around her. And I don't want *her* to take me shopping or anywhere else. I have my own plans for today. I heard you say Tracy was away from the hospital because she was sick. So I'm going over to see how she is. Annie is making some custards to take to her."

"You are not going to see Tracy Ross, and that's final, Cathy." Bert's voice had sharpened; it was an order. "You've been hanging around Tracy entirely too much, running over there every Sunday, carrying tales no doubt, making a general nuisance of yourself."

"Tracy doesn't think I'm a nuisance! She loves me. Nobody else loves me, but Tracy does!"

The silvery voice broke in all sweetness. "Cathy darling, I love you. If only I could make you believe how terribly, terribly anxious I am to lavish love on you, to be a real mother to you!"

"I don't want your kind of love," screamed Cathy, suddenly out of control. "You're simply putting on an act to make a hit with Dad. I only wish he could have seen you the night you threatened me! You know you did. *You did!*"

Because he could not think what else to do, Bert instantly reverted to the stern parent who was to be obeyed. Cathy was to get dressed immediately. She was to spend the day exactly as Fern had planned it.

"I want no more nonsense out of you, Cathy. Now stop your carrying on. Do as you're told."

He left the room, Fern following. In the downstairs hall, she told him, her tone sorrowful: "Darling, I hate to tell you this, because I don't want to add to your burden of worry. But I must tell you. I'm afraid the child is becoming seriously deranged."

"Oh, come now, honey." That, his faintly amused tone implied, was stretching her imagination.

"No," she said, sighing, as if to suggest that she only wished it were her imagination. "When I went into her room, Cathy was on her knees, talking away at a great rate, exactly as if she were talking to another person."

Bert nodded quietly. "She was saying her prayers, Fern, as her mother taught her to do." Grace, he added, had been devoutly religious.

"But this was not praying, Bert. I swear to you. It was – well, like she was holding a conversation with someone she imagined to be right in the room. I heard her tell whoever it was to hurry up, for goodness' sakes. And then she said, 'Well, thanks a million. I know I can depend on you.' Does that sound like a prayer, Bert?"

"Well, I can't say that it does." He frowned, looking thoughtful.

"Oh, darling, why don't you face it? Your child is cracking up mentally. If you don't send her quickly to a place where she can get the help she desperately needs –"

In her room, Cathy stood very still for a moment, her cold hands clenched into tight little fists. Then, biting down hard on her underlip to hold back her tears, she went to get dressed.

Chapter Twelve

It was early when Tracy awakened the next morning, and it was a relief to realize that she felt more like herself again. For a while she lay still, a faint smile on her lips as she thought dreamily about Larry and what had happened just before they had left his house. During the two hours she was there, he had said a lot of things to irritate her, to make her feel that she might be a serious case of emotional immaturity. But he probably hadn't meant half of it. And anyway, it was thinking about those last few minutes that made her feel so warm and good all over.

He wouldn't have kissed her the way he had if he didn't like her, would he?

Why it should make her feel so lovely to know that he liked her was a question she would defer to some other time.

When her mother came in with a tray, wanting to know how she felt, Tracy said cheerfully that she felt marvelous. She sat up, and after she had taken a few sips of hot coffee, she announced that she was going for a walk when she finished breakfast and dressed.

"I left a ring in Cathy's bathroom, and I'm going to walk over and get it."

This was the first Sally had heard of the ring, but she knew her daughter well enough not to ask prying questions. Tracy had always been the kind to keep things to herself, especially when something was preying on her mind.

Now Sally flashed her a glance and remarked: "It's a mile over to Bert Brooks' house. Are you sure you feel up to walking that far, honey? Why not drive over?"

Because she felt restless, Tracy explained.

It was a beautiful morning. A good brisk walk would do her good. She could, she supposed, phone Cathy. But she was anxious to see and feel that beautiful ring back on her finger.

Until she could touch it, look at it, she would feel vaguely uneasy about it.

An hour later, as she walked up the path to Bert's front flagstone patio, the door opened and Cathy came out, accompanied by Annie Barker. The child's eyes lighted as she said hello. Then Cathy added worriedly: "I've got to go to Sunday School. Annie is driving me. But I won't be much more than an hour. Will you wait until I get back?"

"I didn't come for a regular visit, Cathy. I just walked over to pick up the ring I left in your bathroom the other day."

Cathy shook her head. "I didn't see any ring."

Tracy turned to the older woman. "Did you find my ring, Annie? It was a diamond, a large and valuable one."

Annie Barker, whose honesty was beyond question, shook her head firmly. "I went in there to straighten up that afternoon, but I didn't see a sign of any ring. I pledge you my word."

Frowning thoughtfully, Tracy looked back at Cathy, who blurted out: "Maybe Fern

Wilson found it. She was in there not long after you left."

"I wouldn't put it past that one to pick it up and never say a word about it," said Annie.

"Neither would I?" Cathy burst out explosively. But when Tracy wanted to know why she said that, the little girl compressed her lips tightly and shook her head.

"I have my reasons," she said finally. "But please don't ask me what they are. I can't tell you."

Looking both worried and dubious, Tracy was silent for a moment. To be doubtful about Fern Wilson's sanity was one thing. But in all fairness, it seemed unlikely that she was a thief.

"Is your father around, Cathy?"

"He's back in his office," Annie Barker said.

"Alone?"

"No." He was with a patient, Annie explained. A man had just come in with a leg wound. It was bleeding badly, and the doctor was trying to fix the patient up without sending him to the hospital.

"Maybe I can help," said Tracy, and headed around the path toward the office annex.

Bert's patient, an elderly man, was on the

examining table in a back room. Bert was working over him, and when he glanced up and saw Tracy, he exclaimed: "You're the answer to a prayer. Get your coat off; scrub your hands; then come here and help me with this bandage job."

The gash was deep and ugly, resulting from a stack of pine logs toppling over when the old gentleman was getting wood for his fireplace. Tracy could recall the day, during her early training, when she herself would have toppled over, sick as a dog, from the sight of all that blood. But a nurse learned to overcome such squeamishness.

Bert worked with sure, knowing hands, and for the next hour, standing across from him, watching his skillful probing for splinters before bandages were applied, his absorption in preparing the way for nature to do its own healing job, Tracy felt just a hint of the old hero-worship stealing over her.

But when the job was finished and the old man's son had come to drive him home, Bert spoiled it all.

Standing beside the wash basin toweling his hands, he snapped: "Well, my morning is shot, all because an old fool with rubbery legs hasn't the wits to quit outdoor work."

"Accidents can happen to anybody," Tracy said quietly. "And you're a doctor. It's your job to take care of people when accidents happen."

"Well, I get sick of being stuck with these charity jobs. I won't get a cent out of Hen Williams for a solid morning's work. Heck, I'm still sending him bills for pulling his wife through pneumonia. That was two years ago."

Back in the front office, Tracy put her hands lightly on his shoulders. "Bert," she asked gently, "is making money all you think about? Don't you take any pride, get any deep satisfaction from helping the ill and suffering? Aren't these things a great reward in themselves?"

"I regard my work as a business," he said flatly, and discussed at some length all the long, hard years he had spent studying and training. She didn't need to be told how much it cost a man to become a qualified doctor. "Why should he give back the benefit of all he has struggled through – for free?"

Her hands still touching him, Tracy shook her head reproachfully. "What has happened to you, Bert?"

Her tone took on intensity of feeling. What had happened to that brilliant young man in his early twenties who had talked so passionately of becoming a really great doctor?

"You had ideals then, Bert." Maybe, she

mused aloud, it had been all his wonderful ideas, his fine glowing talk, that had caused a little girl to make a hero of him. "I thought you were the most wonderful guy in all this world!"

"You did?"

"Yes," she said, her sigh deep, long-drawn. "I had this little-girl, dreamy idea you might become one of the greatest of the great in the medical profession."

It could have been, she admitted, that this was what had first given her the idea of becoming a nurse. Her smile held pity for the dreaming child she must have been in those long gone days. "I thought how marvelous it would be if I could become a kind of second Florence Nightingale and work beside you, right down through the years."

Silly of her, wasn't it? she added wryly.

"Why, bless you, honey! What a sweet little thing you were to feel that way about me. Imagine!"

Impulsively his arms went around her. His eyes smiled down into hers. His grin was teasing.

"I always knew you had a kind little-girl crush on me. But I never realized you'd built it up so big!" He went on before she could speak: "Is that really the reason you became a nurse, Tracy? All on account of me?"

"I didn't say that," she protested, suddenly angry because he was taking so much for granted.

She was simply trying to explain, she went on coldly, that it seemed a pity he had turned into the kind of doctor who thought chiefly of making money. But – with a shrug – that was his business. She had no right to criticize his motives, and she apologized for doing so.

And, she went on, walking away from him, she must also apologize for returning to his private office after being ordered out.

Swiftly he came to her, taking her arm. "I didn't mean to order you out, Tracy. Heck, honey, I think the world of you. At the hospital, I don't know how we'd get along without you. By the way, I understand you've been sick. All okay now?"

"I think so, yes." If he would kindly let her finish what she had started to say – "The reason I came here this morning –"

The sweet, bell-like voice broke in as the door opened. "Am I intruding again, darling?" asked Fern Wilson, who seemed to be developing a real flair for appearing when Tracy and Bert were in conference.

Tracy turned quickly, said, "Hello, Miss Wilson," and after a moment's thought: "I'm very glad you're here. Maybe you can tell me something about the ring I left in Cathy's bathroom. Did you find it?"

"Ring? What ring are you talking about, my dear?" asked Fern, her pretty face registering puzzlement.

"A diamond ring, Miss Wilson. I left it on the washbasin. Cathy hasn't seen it, and neither has Annie Barker. They tell me you were in there shortly after I left. Are you very sure you didn't pick it up by mistake?"

"Of all the impudent, insulting questions!" snapped Fern. Then, with the speed of light, the sweetness returned to her tone. "I assure you, darling, I haven't seen it. If I had, I would have turned it over to Bert, naturally."

"What's all this about?" Bert asked, baffled. "I didn't know you went about wearing valuable diamonds, Tracy."

After Tracy had explained, he stared at her for a moment, his scowl ominous. Then his glance went to Fern, who was watching him closely, her tone registering deep regret as she told him: "Well, darling, you know what I told you last night. This should prove I wasn't simply imagining something that didn't happen."

For a moment the small office seemed alive with silence.

"Tracy –" when Bert finally spoke, he sounded truly distressed – "what I am about to say isn't easy for me to say. God knows, I don't want to accuse my own child." But now that he knew about the lost diamond ring, he had no alternative.

He reached for a cigarette, lit it with shaky fingers, then said after another moment's hesitation: "Yesterday Fern took my girl on a shopping expedition. Cathy tried to get out of going. In fact, she staged one of her obstreperous, defiant scenes."

"Oh, darling, do get to the point," Fern broke in swiftly with an amused smile. "What he is trying to tell you, Tracy, is simply this. We were in the Five and Ten and I saw the child helping herself to some trashy jewelry which she slipped into a coat pocket."

"I don't believe it!" Tracy snapped instantly.

"I didn't want to believe it, either," said Bert. "But now that I've learned about your ring, what can I believe?"

"That Cathy is a thief," said Fern without hesitation, and in a tone which held undoubted satisfaction. It's just one more proof, darling, that your motherless infant is in desperate need of psychiatric help."

Tracy asked quietly, her eyes on Bert: "Have you found the things your *friend* accuses Cathy of taking?"

"Naturally not," Fern answered for him. "The child has hidden them away and, needless to say, denies the whole thing." Which, she added, was to be expected. Kids invariably lied when they were caught in wrongdoing, didn't they?

"Some children lie," Tracy replied calmly. "Some do not. In Cathy's case, I happen to know that she had a sense of honesty instilled in her by her mother. If she had done something she should not have done, I believe she would have the courage to admit it."

Her glance went to Bert as she said with complete conviction: "I do not believe that Cathy took my ring. What's more," she went on, anger rising in her voice, "since you are her father, Bert, it might be wise for you to show a little trust in Cathy. Wait until you have proof, tangible proof, before you decide that she's guilty."

Even a hardened criminal, she reminded him tartly, was presumed innocent until he was proven guilty.

"Then who could have taken your ring?" inquired Fern. For a moment the eyes of the two girls met squarely, and for the very first time Tracy glimpsed recognition in those long-lashed, violet-blue eyes tangling with hers. Mixed with the recognition was stark hatred.

But the voice was sweetly amused. "If it wasn't Cathy – or dear Annie Barker who we all know is the soul of honesty – then who did take it?"

"You tell me," said Tracy.

Chapter Thirteen

In view of her growing distrust of Fern's mental stability, plus her years of experience with irrational patients, Tracy should never have permitted herself to be alone in a car with the other girl. It was not that she didn't realize, uneasily, that she was taking a chance. But before she could collect her wits she was trapped. That was the way she explained it to herself afterwards.

When she was ready to leave, Bert insisted on driving her home, and Tracy said instantly: "Thank you. I'd appreciate it." She was weaker than she had realized, and in addition, she was anxious to talk to Bert alone about Cathy. Surely there must be some way, some words she could find, to make him understand that he might be doing his little daughter a terrible wrong.

"I could drive her home, darling," Fern put in. Her voice dripped sweetness, but her eyes, meeting Tracy's, were cold and unpleasant. "You don't need to bother."

"No bother at all," said Bert. But just then the phone rang, and after he took the call, he explained that it was the hospital calling him about an emergency case. "Sorry, Tracy. But you know how it is when a child is having convulsions and the mother is positive he's dying. Fern will run you to your house."

What could she do?

"Come along, darling," said Fern, a hint of laughter in her tone. "I know you would have preferred being chauffeured by my handsome doctor. But that's the way the ball bounces."

They hadn't been in Fern's car five minutes before Tracy had the horrible feeling that her life was in jeopardy.

To start with, Fern suggested a "nice little drive. How about that, dear?"

And when Tracy firmly refused, saying that she was just out of a sick bed and really wasn't up to driving around, Fern seemed to take what she said as an extremely amusing joke. With a merry laugh: "I'm *so* sorry you've been ill. But this is such a beautiful autumn day. The air's so fresh and crisp. And I'm sure a nice little drive will do you a world of good. So here we go."

"Miss Wilson, please," Tracy tried again, alarm growing in her. Was she at the mercy of an insane woman? she wondered, as the car gathered speed, careening around sharp dangerous curves, heading for the hill country where the highway would be practically deserted, the cliffs at some points steep and deadly.

"Truly I'm not well. I'd appreciate it if you'd take me back."

"I'll bet." The laughter Tracy heard then was high and shrill. "Scared of me, aren't you, sweetie?"

"Why should I be scared of you? I simply want to get home as quickly as possible."

"What's your hurry?"

There was silence for a time, while the foreign-make car continued to climb.

Suddenly Tracy snapped furiously: "I won't stand for this. For the last time, will you kindly turn back? Let me out at the first public phone booth, and I'll call for a cab."

"Sorry, sweetie. I'm afraid you won't be needing a cab after I speak my little piece."

She laughed softly.

"You sound like a crazy woman!" Tracy exclaimed without thinking.

More soft laughter. "That's what you've thought about me right along, isn't it?" And the car continued to climb, then stopped beside a cliff so steep and sharp that it made Tracy a trifle dizzy to look down.

Fern braked the car, produced a pack

115

of cigarettes, offered one to Tracy, who declined, and lit one for herself. Leaning back, she inhaled pleasurably, then exhaled, all the time watching her companion. Her no longer lovely eyes had taken on an expression of devilish cunning.

"Okay," she said finally. "Let's stop playing cat and mouse with each other. You recognized me that first day in the drugstore. Didn't you?"

"I'm not sure what you mean."

"You're a rotten liar, Tracy." Fern tossed the half-smoked cigarette out the window, and Tracy exclaimed involuntarily: "You shouldn't do that. It could start a fire."

"So it could, sweetie. But don't you worry your head about what might happen to the flora and fauna in these old hills. You've got your hands full worrying about what's going to happen to you. See?"

Tracy could not make up her mind exactly what she was up against. Was this a secondary personality abruptly taking over in the case of a girl who was basically schizophrenic? Or was it simply a scheming, ruthless girl showing her true colors?

"Listen, sweetie," Fern went on. "This little old Southern town isn't big enough to hold you and me both. That's what I brought you up here on the mountain top to tell you."

116

Tracy did an abrupt about-face.

She spoke calmly, managing to keep her voice friendly. "I should think you'd realize by now that you have nothing to fear from me, Fern."

"So you've finally gotten around to a first-name basis." More soft laughter. "That's a switch. But don't bother getting all buddy-buddy with me at this late date. It won't work, sweetie."

Tracy went on determinedly, "I'll admit I recognized you, but I've kept what I knew to myself. I've never breathed a word about you to Bert Brooks. I didn't feel that I had the right."

"But it's been troubling your conscience like mad, hasn't it?"

"Never mind about my conscience. What I knew about you was confined to our nurse-and-patient relationship. I knew that you had been dismissed from that hospital as cured. So, for professional reasons, I felt that my lips were sealed. Can't you believe that?"

"Sealed lips. You've sure got a funny way of talking, sweetie. Nurse-and-patient relationship. Big deal."

She tossed out a second cigarette and leaned toward Tracy. "Now I'll tell you a few facts, sweetie. First and foremost, I don't trust you as far as I can throw you. Sooner or later – and

117

probably sooner – that little old conscience will get the best of you. Then your sweet little sealed lips will come unsealed – and I'll get thrown back to the wolves. I'm not about to wait for that to happen."

"Will you please listen to me, Fern? I have no desire to cause you any trouble. I know what it means for a one-time mental patient to go back to the world, stuck with the stigma of insanity. I know how cruel people can be, how intolerant. That's one reason I've kept what I know to myself. The doctors said you were cured."

"Which just goes to show I learned how to play their game! I put one over on those smarty-smart psychiatrists. If you think I've come this far, just to be licked by a mealy-mouthed little nincompoop of a nurse, better think again, sweetie."

Tracy's eyes registered faint surprise. "Surely you aren't claiming you were *not* cured."

Fern made a gesture of exasperation. "Frankly, I don't know whether I was cured or not. As they say in those joints –" her tone was mocking – "despite the emotional conflicts suffered by this patient, the prognosis in her case is good. She has shown steady and definite improvement."

Oh, sure, she was improved.

"I learned the rules of the game," she announced triumphantly.

"All I wanted was to play the game the way they wanted me to play it and get out of that hell-hole. So that's what I did."

She had, Fern continued, pretended to take the analysis sessions very much to heart. She had learned, as they say, to co-operate, and to watch her every word and move, to prove that she was becoming more and more adjusted every day in every way.

"And it worked!"

As she went on, Fern's talk sounded like shrill, wild ranting. But it isn't, thought Tracy, recalling a conversation with one of the hospital psychiatrists.

"When we dismiss a patient as cured," he had said, "we can never be sure about the chances of a permanent cure." Then he had used a favorite phrase of his own. *When we reach their hearts, the chances are very good.*

"But when they only learn to understand their problems intellectually, not so good. If there is no deep character change, the chances are we'll get them back again."

"So I was smart enough to get out! I was smart enough to come where I wasn't known, come up with a plausible story, then get things set up for exactly the kind of life I want. I'll marry a rich doctor. And then if I blow my stack again, hubby will have to look after me. Except for the brat, I've really got it made. And I'm working on that. So what have I got to worry about?"

She had been shouting.

Abruptly her tone lowered to little more than a whisper. Her face had sharpened to ugliness. "Only you! You, sweetie, are the one and only person who could louse up all my lovely plans. So –"

Swiftly her hand moved to her bag. Another swift movement, and Tracy was staring at a small pearl-handed revolver which was pointed straight at her.

Never let a psycho know you are afraid. Recalling that basic rule from her early psychiatric training, Tracy fought the panic rising inside her.

"Don't you realize," she asked quietly, "that if you kill me, you'll be found out? You'll be locked up a in a jail cell. No doubt you could plead insanity, but what good would that do you? You'd be sent to a place for the criminally insane. Think that over."

Fern looked amused. "Listen, sweetie. Like I just told you, I was smart enough to put it over on the docs and nurses in that hellish loony-bin. Then I was smart enough to come to this neck of the woods, where nobody had ever heard of me, and put on an act that fooled the whole blasted town. If you think I couldn't fool a jury of dopey Southern gentlemen with all their reverence for womanhood – especially beautiful blonde womanhood – *keep your hand off that door!*" she shrilled, as Tracy made a quick move.

The little revolver nuzzled her chest, and Tracy, curiously calm, able to think clearly, did a sudden shrieking act of her own. "There's a car heading straight for us! Look! Around that curve –"

Involuntarily Fern's eyes swiveled. Only for a second, but that second was all Tracy needed to get her hand around the soft, pretty hand which held the gun. After that, she had all that she had learned as a psychiatric nurse going for her. The strength in her fingers was the strength of steel. The trick she had learned through practice, how to twist and hold helpless the arm of a deranged patient, now proved worth more than gold. It was worth her life.

Forced to release the revolver, Fern gave a cry of venomous anger as Tracy pitched it out through the car window, toward the emptiness beyond the mountain cliff.

For the next few minutes Fern fought like an enraged tigress, clawing, tearing at Tracy's hair, long nails gouging deep into her cheek, until Tracy was forced, in self-defense, to land a blow on the beautiful blonde head.

Then Tracy opened the car door, gave one last glance at her stunned companion, and seconds later was running down the curving highway as if she were pursued by a demon.

Chapter Fourteen

In his office, Larry Sizer sat at his desk, going through the motions of studying case records, reminding himself at regular intervals to keep his mind on what he was doing. Once before he had allowed himself to become emotionally involved with a girl to the point where it was hard for him to think of anything else. She had become close to an obsession with him. And what had come of all the fine rapture, of his dreaming belief that he had found his one and only great love?

Yeah, what!

It was a good question to put to himself every so often, a good safeguard against making the same mistake again.

Disillusionment – disillusionment of the first order.

That was what had come of his great romance.

Leaning back in his chair, Larry closed his eyes. His inner ear seemed to hear a voice. It came very clearly, words echoing down the corridor of time.

"The trouble with you, Larry dear," drawled the voice, "is that you're an incurable romanticist. You're so romantic about your work that it's nauseating. Take all this fine talk about how you'd rather give your skill to a penniless woman dying of cancer than to an old gal with millions who wants a doctor's care and attention for kicks. It's so impractical, dear. Oh, sure, like you say, somebody should help the pitiful old pauper. But why does it have to be you?

"And of course," came the echoing words from that moment, long gone, which marked the blasting of his dreams, "when it comes to little girls, you've simply never learned what they're made of. Sugar and spice and all things nice! Well, honey, up to a point, I'd say that was a perfect description of *me*. But since I'm that nice, why shouldn't I demand a lot of nice things in return, such as a devoted hubby who will realize that it's his duty to make lots and lots and lots of nice money, to buy his darling all the cars and jewelry and furs and gadgets that her selfish little heart desires? You *do* see what I mean, don't you? You do see that I'd be an idiot to toss away all that I have to offer on a man who expects me to struggle along on a tiny income plus lots of beautiful love. Don't you?"

Larry sighed, opened his eyes, pushed aside his stack of record cards and got up to prowl the room.

I've allowed myself to grow bitter, he mused. Maybe that was a mistake. Just because one girl had proved a great disappointment, it did not necessarily follow that all girls were stinkers of one sort or another. Did it?

He paced, frowned, stretched and yawned. Then he went back and sat down again. If only Tracy Ross weren't so obviously obsessed about her big shot hospital doctor –

Obsessed – there was that word again. Clenching, then unclenching his hands, he considered. Maybe everyone in the world was obsessed about something or other: money, sex, ambition, some darned thing. Maybe it was obsession, not love, that made the world go round. If a man or woman didn't have an obsession handy, the psychiatrist would manage to dig one out in short order, or invent one. And what was wrong with that? A psychiatrist had to live, pay rent, buy food and clothes, support a wife, maybe pay big alimony to an ex-wife, just like any other man.

Maybe I'm going nuts, thought Larry, as his scrambled thoughts seemed to be veering off in a dozen different directions. He sighed. Well, that was what came of listening to the troubles of a beautiful girl, then taking the girl in his arms, and spending the next twelve hours dreaming, both waking and sleeping, about the sweetness and wonder and promise of her responsive lips.

The door opened. Aunt Carrie came in, dressed to the nines in a green outfit, carrying a mink stole.

"Larry love," she scolded, "you've spent the whole morning in here moping. I've been to church, come back, now I'm off again, and I don't believe you've set foot outside this room. What's come over you?"

"Auntie dear," he replied, grinning, "may I ask what's come over *you?* You look as young and pretty as a schoolgirl. You're blushing like a schoolgirl, too. Could it possibly be that the Reverend Mister Paul Keefer shows signs of surrendering to your romantic plans?"

"Such talk!" Aunt Carrie drew up a chair, produced the inevitable cigarette holder and lit a cigarette. Then: "All right, Larry. I'm not the kind of woman who likes to live without a companion. Our minister is a very fine man, and he does seem to be showing a little interest in me. He's been very lonely since his wife died. He has told me that quite frankly, and like myself, he feels he would be happier with some understanding person to share his joys, burdens and sorrows."

Larry's grin widened. "Congratulations, Auntie. I see you've been making real headway. More power to you."

She studied him for a moment, then said very seriously: "Larry, I do wish you'd find the right girl and marry her."

"Let's skip that record." He frowned slightly.

Having heard it so often, he knew the words by heart. Carrie meant well, she had a heart of gold, and in many ways she had been a lifesaver for him. But she did not believe God intended a man to live out his years as a lonely bachelor. She could come up with an astonishing variety of arguments to prove her point.

"Look, darling." An affectionate smile replaced his frown. "What do I need with a wife? Haven't I got you to run the house, take a phone calls and do the marketing?" He sighed lugubriously. "Where would I ever find a girl who could make vegetable soup to equal yours?"

Aunt Carrie was not in the mood for frivolous talk. "All right." She was still quite serious. "At the moment, I keep things running smoothly for you. But suppose I were to marry our minister and move into his house. Then what would you do?"

Leaving him to ponder that worrisome possibility, Aunt Carrie breezed out. Larry resumed his pacing, his expression decidedly gloomy. Without Carrie to look after things, he would be faced with a very real problem. But what the heck! He could always find a housekeeper.

But what about someone waiting for him at the end of a hard day? Someone with soft, eager arms and eyes filled with love. Someone to share little jokes, to comfort him when he was troubled. Someone – the old cliché flashed through his mind – to walk with him, hand in hand, on into the sunset years?

Suddenly he made a harsh sound in his throat. What the devil was wrong with him?

Never before had he given in to this kind of downright maudlin thinking.

Why was he doing it now?

And why was he suddenly seeing, as clearly as if she were there with him, the flash of the most beautiful deep blue eyes in the world?

And why did the thought come to his mind: *She isn't the kind of girl to kiss a man as she did me unless she feels something close to love.*

He shook his head, as if to clear it of confusing thoughts, and then he heard the cab drive up outside.

He went to the door. When he opened it, Tracy was staggering up the walk. Her clothes were torn, there was blood on her cheek, and when she reached him she went into his arms, clutching him.

"Oh, Larry!" she sobbed, sounding nearly hysterical. "She tried to kill me. She almost did."

He would not allow her to talk until he had cleansed her face, given her a tranquillizer, gotten her calmed down and settled on the couch with a hot drink.

Drawing a chair up close, resting a comforting hand on her wrist, he said finally: "Feeling better?"

"A little." She nodded, but her teeth were still chattering as she said: "I've lived, worked among the violently insane." She had faced the horrors of coping with patients who had reverted to the mindless state of enraged wild animals. She shook her head slowly.

"But this was the first time I ever knew the meaning of physical fear." She sighed, pressing her fingers around his hand as if seeking its comforting strength. How she had managed to keep her head, she would never know.

When she found herself streaking along the highway, safe for a few minutes at least, then

128

the frenzy of fear took over.

"All I could think of was getting to you!"

"I'm glad of that, Tracy." How glad she would never understand. He didn't understand it himself, he thought, as he got up to bring her more hot coffee. Then he reminded her that so far she had been a bit incoherent. "So let's start over, honey. Tell me exactly what happened, right from the beginning."

Larry, too, had never known the meaning of physical fear. But he knew it now. For himself, he had no fear of death. But the realization that Tracy's life might have been destroyed in the second of time it took for the careless finger of a mentally disorganized woman to touch a trigger taught him the meaning of sick horror.

When Tracy had finished, then asked him: "What am I to do, Larry?" he said without hesitation: "For one thing, it's time for you to tell Bert Brooks everything you know about his beautiful psycho."

For another, she herself must get out of this town until Fern Wilson was committed back to an institution for the insane. As long as that girl was free to walk the streets of this town, Tracy would be in danger.

"And I," said Larry, "would never know a minute's peace."

For a moment Tracy's eyes met his in wonderment. "But why?"

"Why what?"

"Why should it matter so much to you, Larry? I mean – well, after all, we don't even know each other very well. I've come bothering you with my problems, but that doesn't mean you should worry overtime, thinking I might be shot by a lunatic."

"We'll get around to my reasons later, my girl. Meanwhile, will you promise to do exactly as I say?"

She smiled at him thinly. "You make it all sound very simple, Larry. But what makes you so sure Bert will believe my story even if I do tell him?"

"Why wouldn't he believe you?"

"I'm up against a very clever girl, Larry. It's obvious that she has completely irrational moments, but she is also clever as a fox, as the insane so often are."

And as for her leaving town – Tracy shook her head firmly. Where would she go? What would she do? What explanation would she give her mother so as to not worry Sally to death?

The phone rang.

After Larry took the call and explained to a worried asthma patient that he was tied up with an emergency case, he found his pipe, lit it and paced the floor, lost in thought, for several long minutes.

"I have a plan," he said when he returned to the chair beside the couch.

Shortly after he came to Oakwood, he had invested in a few acres of property a short distance up in the hills. There were three cottages tucked away in the woods. One was a fair-sized, quite livable cottage. Two were little more than shacks. Some day he planned to do some rebuilding, make some additions, and turn the property into a kind of nursing place for recuperative patients. Meanwhile, he used it occasionally as a refuge for himself.

"I think it would be the perfect place for you, Tracy. You could hide away there for the time being. I'll tell your mother you are going there at my orders, to relax after your bout with the flu."

"I hate the idea of running away," Tracy objected. She was feeling much calmer now. As her feeling of panic died away, she began to wonder if her fears and panic were largely shock-induced. Maybe her imagination had blown up the whole thing out of proportion.

And another thing: "I'm needed at the hospital, Larry." There was a critical shortage of nurses. Just because she had been threatened by a neurotic female, it was scarcely any justification for laying down on

131

the job and taking to her heels.

Ignoring his ominous frown, she went on stubbornly. "You know how it is with mental cases. Some compulsion keeps building up until suddenly without warning, they are pushed to the point where they simply have to let off steam. So they do some crazy, irrational thing. Then afterwards –"

Well, it was much like when the steam pressure was released from a boiler. Afterward they seemed as normal as anyone else.

"So you think it's a good idea to wait around until this psycho has another compulsion! Is that your plan?"

"Larry –"

"Oh, shut up. Stop talking nonsense."

His hands came down on her shoulders; his face bent toward her. "You're at the mercy of a girl with a deranged mind. You know that as well as I do. She isn't a nice person to start with. Add it all together, and what do you have?"

"I've been trained to understand mentally unstable people, Larry, and to handle them."

"Oh, sure. In a place equipped with padded cells and surrounded by guards and hefty nurses, you know how to hold your own. But what if you're on top of a mountain, with no one but the squirrels and bears to hear your scream for help?"

His glare was ferocious. "Didn't you learn your lesson today?" His hands on her shoulders were savage with outrage, and with his fear for this girl which was like a cold hand clawing at his vitals.

"You came in here looking as if a bear had been ripping at you and shaking with shock. But you seem to have forgotten about that already."

"Maybe I've come to my senses."

"Yeah? Well, you sound more as if you've lost your senses." His breath was hot on her cheek.

"Now let me tell you something, Florence Nightingale. You are *not* going back to the hospital. You *are* going to my hideaway in the woods. You're going because I'm going to take you. And you're going to stay until I decide that it's safe for you to come back. That's the way it's going to be, even if I had to get old Dr. Roberts to take over my practice, while I come up and stand guard over you."

She looked up at him wonderingly.

"Why should you care so much what happens to me?"

His words came, sounding just a trifle like a savage growl. "Because I've fallen in love with you. That's the only reason I can think of."

"You don't mean that. I just don't believe it."

133

"That makes two of us. I find it hard to believe myself. But the fact remains." Breaking off, he clasped his arms fiercely around her, and to her astonishment, as his cheek pressed hers, the tears she felt were his tears.

His words were a husky whisper. "This much I know for sure. If anything bad happened to you, I couldn't take it. We've met, we've had a few hours together, and I'm in love with you. It makes no sense, but that's the way it is."

As abruptly as he had taken her into his arms, he released her. His words were clipped as he stood up.

"We're wasting time."

The first thing to do was to phone Bert Brooks and get him to come over here right away. "After you tell him your story –"

"No," she objected stubbornly.

Very well. If she didn't care for that idea, then he could call the police. Once the cops heard what she had to tell –

She broke in sharply. Never would she consent to talk to the authorities. That would mean an open scandal, and Bert's name would be brought into it. His romance would make juicy copy for the front pages, and it might even cost him his job at the hospital.

"I can just picture the headlines, Larry.

Hospital Chief of Staff Succumbs to Charms of Ex-Mental Patient."

Her frown was determined. "I couldn't do that to Bert Brooks. I just *couldn't*. It might ruin him."

He strode back to the couch, scowling. "So we're back to your obsession about Bert Brooks again! I take it you're more worried about protecting the guy than about your own life!"

"Oh, Larry, don't think that."

"What do you expect me to think?"

"Okay." After a moment's tense silence, she gave in meekly. "If you think I should talk to Bert, phone him to come over."

"Good. That's one step in the right direction." And Larry crossed the room to the phone.

A few minutes later he turned back. "He'll be here in about twenty minutes." Then he got his bag, said that he was on his way to make some house calls, and left her to wonder exactly how she was going to tell Bert the things that she must tell him. And would he believe her?

And what about the things Larry had said to her? Was she to believe that he really and truly loved her? How could she believe that? And even if she did believe it, what then? Was it possible that she was falling in love

135

with Larry? Did she *want* to be in love with Larry Sizer?

Around and around went the baffling questions.

Did he? Didn't he? Did she? Didn't she? Was her life really in danger? Or wasn't it? And what was Bert's reaction going to be? Would he believe her story, which was bound to come as a terrific shock? Or would he accuse her of making up a lying story out of whole cloth?

Questions without answers, pressing and pressing until she wondered if her brain might explode. Then she tried to shut them all out of her mind.

There was nothing to do but wait and see what happened.

Chapter Fifteen

As soon as Tracy left with Fern, Dr. Bert Brooks set off for the hospital. But before he had driven very far, he slowed the car to a standstill and sat for a moment lost in scowling thought. Then he wheeled around, heading back for the house and the phone in his office.

Having arranged for a resident doctor to take over his emergency case, Bert went around to the house proper. He went straight upstairs to Cathy's room. His face wore an expression of frowning uneasiness. He was a deeply disturbed man. *Had his child turned into a little sneak-thief?*

He didn't want to believe that.

Heaven knew he didn't want to believe it.

He loved the kid. Maybe he wasn't much of a hand at showing his love. Grace used to say that he should make more of an effort to communicate with his little girl.

"Why don't you take Cathy for little walks in the woods, darling? Talk with her. Tell her about the wild flowers, explain to her about the wonders of nature. Get to know her. She's your child, Bert. She's part of your flesh. I'm sure you do love her deeply. But you must make her understand about your love. If you don't establish a very real and deep bond now, you'll never do it. She'll grow up feeling as if you were a stranger who doesn't care very much about her."

For a moment he hesitated in front of Cathy's dressing table. He picked up the small portrait in the oval silver frame. Grace's lovely dark eyes looked back at him. Their gaze seemed grave and somehow reproachful. Or was that simply his vague sense of guilt?

137

Listen! He spoke silently back to the portrait.

Maybe I wouldn't rate any medals as an understanding father. Maybe I've made all the mistakes in the book. But when you were here – heck, I didn't have the time for little walks. And I didn't know how – I truly didn't know how to talk the kid's language. When I tried, I'd get embarrassed. To tell the truth, I was a little scared of her. So I left the raising of her up to you, and when you died I was struck with a job I didn't know how to handle. But I do love the kid. Honest I do, Grace.

Do you? He could have sworn those dark, reproachful eyes were asking the question.

He sighed, replaced the picture on the table, and turned toward the chest of drawers on the far side of the room. Forcing his thoughts determinedly away from Grace, he concentrated on the matter at hand.

Loving a child because she was his child was one thing. It was an emotional thing. But if she was turning into a thief, in addition to her recent lying, of which he was convinced, it all added up to exactly one thing.

It meant that Cathy was a pre-psychotic type and must be dealt with as such. This was a problem for his intelligence to deal with, not his emotions.

If the kid had taken to snitching cheap

jewelry from department stores, then adding to the loot a valuable ring left accidentally by Tracy, the stuff would be hidden somewhere in her room. He meant to find it.

It's my duty to get at the bottom of this, he assured himself, and proceeded to root through the drawers of the chest which contained all of Cathy's personal things.

The diamond ring and the pieces of cheap jewelry, fastened to squares of paper cardboard, were tied in a silk scarf which had been her mother's. They were hidden in the bottom drawer, under a pile of sun suits which had been laundered and laid away for another summer.

"Oh, my God!" Bert muttered, laying the glittering pieces out on the bed just as the door opened.

"What are you doing in my room, Daddy?"

Turning, he met Cathy's eyes, which, for the moment, showed nothing other than surprise.

Bert took a deep breath, trying to suppress the rage which flooded through him. *His* kid was no better than those delinquent hoodlums you were forever reading about in the papers. When it happened to other people's kids, you thought about it for a minute, scowled, wondering what the world was coming to, then went on to the next sensational story.

But when your own child was involved – "Come here," he said sternly, beckoning Cathy toward the bed. "What is the meaning of this?"

"Of what, Daddy?"

She came slowly, her eyes showing the fear that was becoming her constant companion.

His voice sharpened. "This junk you had hidden away, junk that you stole." He held up a card clipped with ten-cent earrings.

"And this!" He picked up Tracy's ring. "A stone worth a thousand dollars – maybe more. Tracy left it in your bathroom. Why didn't you tell her you had it? Don't just stand there staring, as if you lost your wits. I want the truth out of you, young lady. I want it fast. You did steal it, all of it. Didn't you?"

"I did not. I never saw any of it before."

"Stop lying to me."

"I am not lying. I'm *not*."

"It was hidden away in that bottom drawer. How did it get there?"

"I don't know."

"I suppose the stuff walked there. Is that what you expect me to believe?"

She backed a step away from her father. Her voice was shaky with helpless anger, with frustration. "I can't help what you believe. I never saw any of it before. If it was in that drawer, somebody else put it there. I didn't."

He strode close to her, grabbing her arm. His hand was not gentle. His eyes were totally accusing. "You little liar! You sneaking little thief? All I can say is, thank God your mother didn't live to see what you're turning into. At the rate you're going, you'll end up a common criminal."

Bert had lost all control over himself.

At the mention of her mother, Cathy's eyes flooded with tears. Sobs choked her voice. "If my mother were here, she'd believe me. She *loved* me. She knew I wouldn't lie or steal or anything."

Then she tore away from his gripping hand. Throwing herself across the bed, she burst into a storm of tears. "Oh, Mother," she cried, why did you have to go away and leave me?" She bit at the pillow, whimpering like a hurt animal. "Mother, Mother, I need you so. I'm so alone."

Bert stood over her. His voice was slightly more controlled, but stern. "Stop that crying," he ordered. "Sit up. Do you hear me, Cathy? I said to sit up."

She sat up.

She wiped away tears with the back of her hand. And the eyes that looked back at him were suddenly too hard, too defiant in their anger, for the eyes of such a little girl.

"I'll tell you who swiped that stuff from

141

the Five and Ten. I wasn't going to tell you, because Mother always told me it wasn't right to 'tell on' other people. But now I've got to tell. Fern Wilson took it. I saw her through a mirror when she didn't know I was watching.

"And," she went on before he could interrupt, "She took Tracy's ring. She must have. Then she hid it in my drawer so I'd get the blame. It had to be that way." In a small, tormented voice, she made one last appeal: "Please believe me, Daddy."

He didn't believe her.

He paced the floor, thinking hard.

Finally he said, coming back to the bed where she still sat, looking tormented and lost: "There's only one thing to do about you, Cathy. It's my duty as your father to see that you get professional help for your problems."

Cathy, broke in, her voice small and hopeless. "My problem is that I haven't anybody to love me or believe a word I say."

"I don't want to hear any more of that talk."

"Well, I don't want to hear any more about how I'm a liar and a thief, when I'm not. I'M NOT!" Her voice rose to a scream.

"Shut up!" It was then that he slapped her face.

Shocked, she stared back at him. No one

142

had ever hit her before.

"If I were a psychiatrist," he said, "possibly I could give you the psychotherapy you need. But I'm not trained along that line. So you will have to be sent to someplace where –"

"I won't go!" she broke in shrilly.

"You'll go where you're sent," he said flatly.

But first she must return these items which did not belong to her to their rightful owners. As soon as they could get in touch with Tracy over the phone, Cathy must confess that she had kept the ring. "You will tell her how sorry you are and ask her forgiveness."

Cathy stared back at him, saying nothing.

"And first thing tomorrow morning, you will go to the store where these other baubles came from. I'll go with you. We'll see the manager; you will return his property and explain that you realize how wrong it was to take it. Is that clear?"

"I won't confess to things I never did. You can't make me."

Bert bent toward her, trying to make his voice calm. "Cathy, please try to understand me. I'm your father, and I'm trying to do what's best for you. You're a very mixed up little girl. You need professional help. But first you must face the fact that you have done a very wrong thing. You must confess that wrong and face the music. Don't you understand?"

Her eyes blazed. "I understand just one thing. Fern Wilson wants to marry you, but she doesn't want to be bothered with me. She's told you all kinds of lies about me. Now she's *framed* me – pushing herself into my room after I've told her and told her to stay out, then hiding things in my drawer that *she* stole. It's like she was setting a trap, and I'm caught in it."

Suddenly she cried out: "What am I to do? Oh, Mother, what am I to do!"

"Stop it!" Again the angry hand hit her cheek.

He had told her what she was to do. He wanted no more argument about it. She was to stay in her room and think things over.

"And here you will stay, young lady, until you are ready to tell the truth and confess your guilt."

Cathy said: "Then I'll stay here forever."

Bert shut the door, locked it from the outside, and went back to his office. He was too weary, too confused and upset to think straight. But he had to think.

For a long time he sat at his desk, both Grace and Fern Wilson in his thoughts. No two women could have been more different, yet both had aroused a very deep love in him. Or was love the right word? Maybe each, in her own way, had satisfied a great and urgent need.

With Grace, the need had been for someone to depend on. "Emotionally, you're still a child, Bert." Tracy's accusing words flashed through his mind. Cringing inwardly, he assured himself that it was a lie. He was *not* a mama's boy; he had *not* used Grace as a mother. Marriage was intended to be a sharing, wasn't it? So what had been wrong with Grace sharing the burdens, looking after the problems which he had not the time for?

Still, he did wish that Grace was there to decide what to do about Cathy. Strangely, too, he found himself wishing for the comfort and peace he had always found in Grace's arms.

It was this kind of love, in full measure and running over, that Grace had always given him. With Fern – well, with her love represented something quite different.

Excitement? Passion? The urgent cry of his senses for a kind of ecstasy he had never known before?

With a hoarse sob, he buried his face in his arms, and the cry inside him was the helpless cry of an infatuated man completely under the spell of a fascinating girl.

His whispered words were broken.

"Whether she's right or wrong about sending the kid away, that's what she wants. And I'll have to do it. I can't help myself."

He sat there, head buried, shoulders hunched over, for a long, long time.

How long he didn't know. Suddenly the door flew open and Fern stood there, her face paperwhite.

"Look," she said, throwing off the coat which draped her shoulders as she came toward him.

She held out one arm. It was covered with blood from wrist to shoulder. "Tracy Ross came at me with a knife," she explained. She was curiously calm.

"And look at this," she said, touching the bruise and swelling on her forehead, the flesh all around it an angry, purplish black.

"The idiot went berserk and tried to kill me," Fern said. "She hit me in the head with a rock."

Chapter Sixteen

As soon as Larry left, Tracy did what she could to make herself look presentable. She bathed her face again, swabbed peroxide on the cut place on her cheek, combed her black hair to its customary sleek neatness. One sleeve of her loosely knit pink sweater had been ripped to shreds by Fern's clawing fingers, but she managed to knot some of the loose ends of wool together. All the time her busy fingers moved, she was trying to think coolly and clearly.

Exactly how was she going to go about telling Bert the truth about Fern? What was the right approach?

Through the window she saw his car stop in front of the house. She opened the door as he came up the path.

For a brief moment they stared at each other, not speaking.

"Where's your hypnotist friend?" Bert asked as he walked in, glanced around, then frowned at Tracy in what she considered a singularly strange way.

"Larry had to leave to visit several patients."

"No one else in the house?"

"No."

"Good." He sat down stiffly, avoiding Tracy's eyes as he said: "What I have to say, to talk over with you, is anything but pleasant for me. It had best be said in private."

Tracy sat down, her frown puzzled as she stared at him. "I have something very

147

unpleasant to tell you, Bert. But I didn't imagine you would know about it before I told you. *Do you know?*"

He drew a long, difficult breath, and the words seemed to come hard. "What I know, Tracy, is simply this. Today you obviously cracked up and tried to murder Fern Wilson. You may thank your lucky stars that you didn't succeed. After she regained consciousness, she was able to make her way to my office. After she told me what had occurred, I was about to call the police. It was Fern herself who stopped me. She advised me not to be hasty. She seemed to feel that there might be extenuating circumstances."

As he talked, Tracy had the feeling that she was listening to words spoken by an actor in a play. Momentarily she wondered if Bert could be drunk and actually not understand what he was saying. But of course he wasn't.

He believed every word he was saying.

And as this realization hit her, Tracy gave way to sudden and almost hysterical laughter. This kind of thing did happen, she knew: a mentally deranged personality attempting to accuse another person of insanity. Sometimes they even got away with it, for a little while.

"Tracy, please try to calm yourself, my dear."

"But I can't." And her uncontrolled

148

laughter went on. "This is so ridiculous."

"No, Tracy." He spoke stiffly, but unkindly. "There is nothing ridiculous to laugh at. What you did was a desperately serious matter. Surely you realize that." He studied her with honestly worried eyes. "Or is it possible that you don't *remember* your brutal attack on Fern?"

Regaining control of herself, Tracy looked at him steadily. "No, Bert. I do not remember anything of the sort. What I do remember –"

He interrupted sharply. "Do you mean to sit there and tell me you don't recall slashing Fern's arm in ribbons with a knife you had in your bag?"

"Or," he continued, "bashing her head with a rock?"

"Did I really do all that?" Tracy could not resist flinging the mocking words at him. "And she lived to get back to your office and tell the sad tale?" With a wondering shake of her head: "The gal must be made of cast iron."

But it all fits into a pattern, she thought, as her thoughts ran back to that night when Fern had been dragged up to the violent ward. That was the night she had slashed her wrist with a piece of jagged tin and pounded her head against a wall.

Bert was talking on, quietly and calmly, as

149

a man talks who is offering to do a great favor if the other person is willing to co-operate.

"What I want to say is just this."

In view of their long friendship, dating back to Tracy's childhood, he would be willing to protect her in every way possible. He had, he said, always felt toward her much as if she were a little sister, and he was ready to admit that she had been under a great strain recently, trying to do the work of two or three nurses, working around the clock, and so on.

"And I'm taking into consideration the years you put in as a psychiatric nurse, Tracy."

That in itself, he conceded, was enough to make any sensitive, high-strung girl crack up ultimately. He had even known of psychiatrists who, to use the slang expression, went around the bend as a result of spending all their working hours around psychotics.

"It isn't to be wondered," he conceded generously, "that you've finally reached the breaking point. Now here's what I suggest."

Tracy interrupted abruptly. "Just as a matter of curiosity, would you care to tell me exactly why I made this attack on your girl friend?"

He looked embarrassed. "According to Fern, you said that you had been in love with me for years. Let's put it this way. You have made a kind of fantasy hero of me. You don't want me to ruin my life by marrying the wrong girl."

Tracy broke in sharply: "And I say *she* would ruin your life. Right?"

"That's about it."

Suddenly Tracy was on her feet. "Well, she certainly told the truth when she said that. Now suppose you listen to me for a minute, Bert Brooks. Larry Sizer insisted that I tell you the real truth about your precious blonde beauty. That's why he phoned you to come here. You won't like what I'm going to tell you, but neither do I like being accused of attempted murder by the woman who threatened me with a gun, and who I know positively to be a mental case."

Bert sat quietly, a faintly amused smile on his lips, as Tracy told him of Fern's record in the mental institution.

Watching his face, Tracy was baffled. There was no trace of shock in his expression, not even surprise.

This, she thought, is really the limit. Was he so bewitched by Fern's beauty and charm that he didn't care? Didn't he consider a deranged mind of great importance? It was unbelievable.

"Do you understand what I am telling you, Bert? I was on duty the night Fern Wilson

151

was dragged, kicking and screaming, into the violent ward. I helped fasten her into the cold pack. You do know what the cold pack is, don't you?"

"Oh, yes." Bert nodded, still with that amused smile.

"Why," she demanded, "do you sit there with that downright imbecilic grin? Don't you grasp what all this means?"

He lit a cigarette, smoked calmly for a moment, apparently as unmoved by her story as if he had been listening to the babbling of a child.

"Are you all finished?" he asked finally.

If she was, he would explain to her why her story didn't mean a thing.

She stared at him, shocked. She sat down. Now, she decided, she had seen love at its best – or worst. She wasn't sure which.

"Fern isn't a mental case," he said firmly. "She never was." As for her little sojourn in that mental institution, this came as no surprise to him. She had told him all about it.

"She went there to get first-hand material for a book she wanted to write."

"Book?" Tracy said vaguely.

Yes. She did know what Fern was a writer, didn't she? He was very sure he had mentioned this at one time or another.

Uncrossing his legs, then recrossing them,

Bert proceeded to explain how for some years Fern had been greatly interested in mental illness. Some friend of the family had been psychotic. While she was still very young, Fern had heard talk about how this friend had been mistreated in the hospital where she was sent. Being still at a highly impressionable age, Fern had developed a passionate desire to do her bit to make sure the institutions where such people were hospitalized were properly run.

"So she got the idea of writing a book about such a place," Bert said, the earnestness in his voice showing that he believed every word he was saying.

Silent, Tracy stared at him.

"But in order to write such a book, she wanted to get first-hand information."

In other words, if pitiful, helpless victims of mental disorders were being subjected to brutal treatment by sadistic nurses and guards who treated them like animals, she wanted to find out and write it up. But she did not want to write of horrors and cruelty that were not realistic, simply for the sake of sensationalism.

Bert lit a fresh cigarette. "And so Fern arranged to have herself committed to such a place, posing as a patient."

"Just like that, eh?" Tracy's short laugh

was humorless. "Exactly how did she go about it? Just walk in, say, 'I'd like to be committed as a lunatic, please,' and will you please proceed to shoot the works?"

She gazed at him, incredulous.

"Surely you don't believe such nonsense, Bert." She tried to explain to him that this simply was not done. "Truly, Bert, nobody orders extended mental treatment the way they'd order a meal in a cafeteria." It wasn't quite that simple.

He seemed to believe that it was. Under given circumstances, that is. In Fern's case, she knew a prominent, very fine psychiatrist who had been a long-time friend of her father's. At her request, this man had certified her as needing psychiatric treatment, and that was the way she worked it.

Again there was that trace of pity in his smile.

"So you see, my dear, now that you know the real explanation, it doesn't leave much to your story. Does it!

"Obviously not."

Not, that is, if one was idiotic enough to believe such a far-fetched yarn.

Having worked in the hospital in question, she didn't believe a word of it. In fact, she added, only an unbalanced mind could dream up such nonsense, or expect an experienced doctor to swallow it.

"How can you swallow it, Bert?"

She was thankful when the phone rang. Crossing the room to answer it gave her a moment to collect her thoughts.

Chapter Seventeen

Tracy lifted the receiver, said hello, then gave a vast sigh of relief when she heard Larry's voice.

"How are things going?" he asked.

"Well –" she hesitated, hunting for words that would let him know she needed him – "there's one emergency. Come as fast as you can, said the caller."

She held her breath, wondering if he would get the message.

He got it.

"Be there in five minutes," Larry said.

The line went dead, and she turned back to Bert, who was on his feet, his face a thundercloud.

"I take it that was your hypnotist friend," he said, moving toward the door. "So I'll be on my way."

She stood in front of him, blocking his way.

"You aren't going anywhere just yet," she said flatly. "and if you have any sense at all, you'll stop referring to Dr. Sizer as a hypnotist."

Not, she added, that there didn't seem to be a nice little job of hypnotism under way. "You're the one who seems to be in a hypnotic trance." And obviously Larry Sizer had had nothing to do with it.

"That girl *must* have you hypnotized, Bert." That, she added, was the kindest explanation of his wild and completely irrational talk.

"Stand aside, Tracy," he said stiffly, as she planted herself firmly against the door to prevent his leaving.

He would, he said, go into more detail later about the ugly mess she had gotten herself into. Perhaps at her own home this evening. Meanwhile, she might be considering whether she preferred to resign from the hospital, pleading ill health, or –

She broke in sharply. "Or be fired? Is that the alternative you're offering me?"

"I'm afraid so." He sounded truly regretful. "As to what your next step had better be –"

She interrupted again. "How about shipping me off to some loony-bin," her tone was mocking, "along with Cathy?"

Her words reminded him of something. Bert reached in his pocket for the diamond ring, which he placed in her hand with the terse comment: "Sorry to have to brand my own child as a thief, but –" he sighed deeply – "I found this hidden in Cathy's room."

Tracy looked at the ring as she turned it in her palm before slipping it on. Then her eyes lifted to this man whom, as a child, she had loved dearly. I used to think of him, she remembered, as a kind of Greek god.

Now, at this moment, she felt a sick contempt for him, mixed with hot anger. How could she not be angry?

On the say-so of a scheming, irrationally evil woman, he was ready to convict her of a heinous crime. No judge and jury required. Fern Wilson's trumped up story was good enough for him. So he would kick Tracy out of her profession, deprive her of her means of livelihood, ruin her life. That was what it came down to. And yet – she felt obscurely sorry for him.

How could you help feeling sorry for a man so under the spell of a girl with a sick, twisted mind that he himself was driven to act and talk like a psycho?

He was trying to force her away from the door. "For the last time, Tracy, please stand aside. I have no intention of discussing my private affairs in front of Sizer."

"*Your* private affairs?" Her laugh was

157

mirthless. "Pardon me if I'm wrong, but I understood we were discussing *me*, and whether or not I had suddenly turned into a psychopathic killer, and whether or not I should be allowed to continue wearing my R.N. cap and pin."

"Tracy, I have no desire to hurt you, believe me. This whole thing has come as a terrific shock to me. In fact, I have so much on my mind that I'm beginning to wonder if I'm going crazy."

"I'm beginning to wonder about that, too, Bert."

He brushed the back of his hand across his eyes. "First I have to cope with the problem of Cathy, who obviously is becoming incorrigible. Now there's you." He shook his head as if in disbelief.

"I'd have said you were as level-headed, as well adjusted, as any girl could possibly be. I've never worked with a finer nurse. That you should crack up – you, of all people!" Another deep sigh.

"But facts must be faced."

"That they must," Tracy agreed amiably. "But when the facts we're facing have to do with my sanity and whether or not I have the makings of a maniac-killer, I prefer to have a witness on hand to hear my side of the story. So you might just as well go back

158

and sit down, Bert. As I said, you aren't going anywhere at the moment. Would you care for a cup of coffee while we wait for Larry?"

Bert did not care for any coffee, thanks just the same.

Nor, when Larry Sizer came and politely and graciously suggested a highball all around, did Bert care for any whiskey. Then he changed his mind about the drink. Perhaps he could use one. "I'm not quite myself, Sizer," he said apologetically as his obviously shaky hand accepted the tall, cool glass.

He had, he explained, been through a series of shocks. He managed a small laugh. And a man could stand just so much.

"That's right," Larry agreed, drawing up a chair close to the hassock where Tracy was sitting. "Every man has his breaking point." He smiled at Tracy, the smile warm and intimate, his eyes filled with understanding.

For a few moments a casual observer might have taken them for three casual friends, enjoying a casual late afternoon drink. But the strain of such phony make-believe was soon too much for Tracy to take.

Setting her glass on the floor, she came out abruptly with the blunt, brutal truth. "Larry, our friend here has accused me of attacking his girl friend with a knife. Then I bashed her skull in – or tried to – with a rock. So he says.

159

He says it must be true, because his beloved says it's true. What do you think of that?"

Larry thought, so he said, that it was a very poor joke. Naturally he assumed that it was a joke. "What am I supposed to do?" he asked pleasantly. "Split my sides laughing?"

But as he spoke his eyes met Tracy's, and they seemed to be saying to her: "I'm taking this easy until I find out what this story is all about."

"I assure you it's no joke." Bert spoke stiffly. "And I'd like to say first, I was thoroughly against dragging you into this unpleasant discussion. I have my pride about such things. Heaven knows, I've always had the highest regard for Tracy. In a sense, you might say that I love her very dearly, like a sister, so to speak. And so, naturally, what happened today has come as a dreadful shock."

"I see," said Larry, and he reached out his hand to cover Tracy's. "Well, I love the gal, too, Doc, only not as a sister. The way I love her –" Interrupting himself, he stood up abruptly, his jaw thrust out, his eyes cold and threatening.

"The way I love her," he repeated, "if any man said to me that she went berserk and tried to kill another human being, I'd knock him down. And I'd keep on knocking him

160

down until he crawled to her on his knees and took every word of it back."

He was breathing hard. "Do I make myself clear, Doc? I am suggesting, if you have any foul accusation to make against Tracy, that you stand up like a man and make it to me. Or do you prefer to start eating your words?"

Bert sat silent, scowling.

"Hold everything, Larry," Tracy broke in swiftly. "You've heard only half of this fabulous drama from real life."

"There's more?"

"Tracy, shut up." Bert's tone was close to an angry growl. "I'm warning you. I will not permit you to discuss Fern's past with this fellow."

"You mean her past in that mental institution?" Larry asked, smilingly. "I already have the low-down on that, Doc. I've known for some time that the blonde was a psycho."

"But she isn't." Tracy looked up at Larry, her smile strange. "She isn't really a psycho. Not according to Bert. The reason she was in the mental hospital was that she personally arranged to go there. She *wanted* to go. See what I mean?"

"Sure. I take it she went for a kind of rest cure. She was worn out by the social whirl and wanted to get away from it all. So a loony-bin seemed the ideal place to rest and relax and maybe do a bit of meditating."

Suddenly his jocular tone changed, hardened, as he leaned down and grabbed Bert by the shoulders. "Listen," he snapped, after Tracy had sketched in the details. "You call yourself a doctor, don't you?"

"Take your hands off me!" Looking utterly furious, Bert was on his feet.

"I asked you a question. You call yourself a doctor, Brooks. You are chief of staff at a small but very good hospital. Generally speaking, you are considered a first class man, a competent surgeon. All this being true, can you actually be ignorant enough, fool enough, to believe a person can be committed for insanity if she is in fact not insane?"

"Fern arranged the whole thing with this psychiatrist," Bert explained. "A very eminent psychiatrist," he added. "A close friend of the family."

"I see. And do you seriously believe that any professional man of standing would lend his name to such a phony hoax?"

"I happen to believe that, yes."

"And do you believe that any sane girl would put herself through the horrors that go on in such a place? Allow herself to be analyzed, shocked, jolted, strapped down, attacked by other completely mindless patients, all because she wanted to write some silly book? Can you honestly believe such outrageous, idiotic nonsense?"

"I don't care to discuss it with you, sir," said Bert with considerable dignity. He started for the door, but he didn't get far.

"I haven't finished," Larry snapped, dragging him back with a forceful hand. "Next question: have you made my effort to contact the hospital and check on this absurd story?"

"Since you ask, no. I didn't consider it necessary to check." And furthermore, Bert explained, Fern said that the entire arrangement had been on most confidential basis. It would be most embarrassing to the psychiatrist who had helped her if any questions were asked.

For a moment Larry's expression was one of utter disbelief. He shook his head in bewilderment. "I'm sorry to have to say this," he said finally, "but if you're really serious about all you've said, you have no business accepting patients or working in a hospital."

He went on talking, almost as if he were ruminating to himself, as disturbing thoughts swarmed through his mind. Prescribing for patients, treating them for various ailments, performing major surgery – each time a man did these things, he was allowing the other person to trust his or her life to him.

Again Larry's hand came down hard on the other man's shoulder. His tone was hard, his words both a threat and a command. "I'll give you three days to contact that hospital and check on Fern Wilson's record. If you fail to do that, I'll bring this whole fantastic story out in the open. If I do, you'll be finished as a medical man. I suppose you understand that much, don't you?"

The look Bert gave him was one of concentrated venom. "Damn you," he muttered through gritted teeth.

Then he strode out, banging the door hard behind him.

Chapter Eighteen

At eight o'clock that evening, Tracy and Larry were seated at the table in her mother's cheerful kitchen, while Sally bustled between table and stove, bringing food which neither of them wanted.

"I don't see any sense in Tracy burying herself up in the woods," Sally said flatly, "just on account of a little cold." She kept glancing at Tracy with concern. She had sense enough to know they weren't telling her the whole truth. Something was going on that they were keeping from her. But what?

Was Tracy in danger of some sort? Rack her brains as she might, she couldn't think how that could be. Her girl was a good girl. Never would Tracy do anything that she shouldn't. And Oakwood was a nice quiet little town. The kind of people who made all the trouble in the world these days simply did not live in Oakwood.

Nothing, mused Sally, ever happened there that was out of the ordinary.

There was a pounding on the back door.

Tracy got up to open it, and Cathy Brooks stumbled into her arms. She was sobbing and trembling, and her hands, clutching at Tracy, were as cold as ice. "You told me," she sobbed, "if I was ever in bad trouble, I was to call a cab and come to your house. And here I am. Please don't send me away. Please don't."

"Of course I won't, darling," Tracy said. "But what in the world has happened?"

Her mother took over briskly. There seemed to be a lot of strange goings-on which she didn't understand. But she did know a sick, frightened child when she saw one; a child who needed a warming drink and

165

a chance to get calmed down.

"She'll tell you what's happened after she's had a bowl of hot soup," Sally said firmly, and ordered Larry to bring up a chair for the poor little love.

Between them, they got Cathy settled at the table. And when Sally asked, putting a bowl of steaming chicken soup in front of her, "Are you hungry, sweetheart?" Cathy nodded, and started to cry again.

She hadn't, she said, had anything to eat since breakfast. And her father said she wasn't to have anything until she confessed to something she hadn't done.

"And after I confess," she gulped, "I'm to be sent away to a place where they send crazy people." And so, she explained, she had climbed out of her bedroom window and down the honeysuckle trellis.

"You mean your father had you locked in your room?" Sally asked, her face a thundercloud. She never had cared too much for Bert Brooks. Even as a boy, he had been too handsome for her taste. But she never would have expected him to mistreat his own child.

"Sounds to me like Bert Brooks has lost some of his marbles," she said tersely, and was relieved to see Larry Sizer draw his chair up close to the little girl. She hadn't seen very much of this new doctor Tracy seemed to be taking a fancy to. But what she had seen, she liked. And when she saw how Cathy smiled and instantly took to him, Larry went sky-high in her estimation. Children and dogs had a sure instinct about men. She began to hope that Tracy had, too, and knew a good man when she found him.

Larry put his arm comfortingly around Cathy and began to talk to her. He said that little girls were his favorite people, and he didn't need to be told that she was a very good, very sweet little girl.

No, in response to her question, he did not believe that she had lied about anything, or that she had stolen anything that didn't belong to her. And no, he very definitely did not believe that she needed to be sent anywhere that she did not want to go.

"Your father is a doctor, honey," he said gently. "But sometimes even doctors get wrong ideas and make mistakes. You'll understand better how that can happen when you're older. For right now, just try to put all that out of your mind. Just believe that we love you and want to help you and we'll see you through this trouble."

Cathy gazed at him earnestly. "Are you a doctor, too?"

"Yes, honey." He smiled at her, smoothing

167

back her hair, his fingers noting that her skin was dry and hot. "I'm a doctor, too."

Cathy sighed. "I wish my father was the kind of doctor you are." Then, after a moment's thought: "But what am I to do?" Her small, flushed face grew fearful. "My father will come looking for me; I know he will."

Tracy, who had been silent, thinking hard, suddenly suggested: "couldn't she come along with me tomorrow morning, Larry?" After all, if his mountain cabin was a fairly safe hiding place for her, why not for Cathy?

What was this talk about a hiding place? Sally wanted to know. She was emphatic. What did Tracy have to *hide* from? There was something very mysterious going on, and she was sick and tired of being kept in the dark.

Larry, looking thoughtful, went outside to get his bag from the car. Back in the kitchen, he took Cathy's temperature, noting that it was two degrees over normal. He looked at Tracy, who agreed that the child really should be put to bed before a serious case of flu or whatever developed.

"On the other hand, we could drive up to the cabin tonight," Larry suggested.

Cathy spoke up to say, wherever they were going to take her, please to take her right away, before her father came looking for her.

168

"When he finds me, he'll make me go straight back home." And, sobbing, everything would be worse than ever.

For a moment Tracy was silent, debating the problem in her mind. Was this hiding away in Larry's mountain place really a smart idea, even for herself? She was not completely sold on the plan, except as a refuge for a few days. With Cathy along – what would happen when Bert notified the police that she had disappeared, as he surely would do?

They would start hunting the hills for every conceivable hideaway. If and when the child was discovered with her, in a place belonging to Larry Sizer, what would happen to Larry, to his professional reputation? Suppose he was accused of being an accomplice in a kidnapping?

The very thought made her fearful. She glanced at Cathy, who put down the glass of milk she had been trying to drink. "I feel awful sick," she said, her small voice shaky. "Please don't let him come and get me while I feel like I feel right now."

"We'll start as soon as I can throw a few things in my bag," Tracy said, getting up from the table. She felt unable to cope with any more problems or emotions just now. Tomorrow would be another day. After a good night's sleep, her mind would be clear and, with luck, things would straighten themselves out.

Half an hour later they were on their way in Larry's car, Cathy warmly bundled up in an Indian blanket Sally had wrapped around her.

"I won't tell anybody a thing," Sally promised just before they drove off. She would lock all the doors, barricade herself in the house, and if Bert Brooks came pounding on her door, he could pound until he dropped dead. She still wouldn't let him in or answer any nosy questions.

In less than an hour they were at the cabin, which faced an isolated hill road a short distance off the main highway. "They'll never find us tonight." That was for sure, said Tracy, as she took Cathy's hand and the two followed Larry into the cottage which nestled in a pine grove.

There was one enormous room, with two alcoves providing space for a single bed each, a chair and chest of drawers. At the far end of the big room was a small kitchen equipped with an icebox, some primitive but adequate kitchen tools, and a closet stocked with an astonishing array of canned foods. "There's enough stuff here to feed an army," Tracy marveled, to which Larry replied, grinning:

"Don't tell anybody, but I have a broad streak of the pack rat."

Then he gave Cathy an affectionate push into the bathroom adjoining the kitchen, and told her to get undressed while he got the open fire started. "Then to bed for you, sweetheart, after I take your temperature and give you some pills."

In front of the fire, while they waited for the pine logs to blaze up, Larry took Tracy's hand and told her not to worry. "I don't like to leave you up here alone, honey." But if he were to stay, that could lead to ugly malicious talk which could smear her character and good name.

When Bert discovered that Tracy had disappeared, along with his child, and when he could get no information from Sally – "His next move will be to phone my office, or come there. If he can't locate me, his next move will be to call in the police."

"And come noon tomorrow, it will be all over town that you and I have absconded with his daughter." Tracy swayed slightly toward him and whispered: "Larry, I'm scared."

His arms closed quietly around her. "So am I," he confessed. "When I think of the very real danger you may be in, with that idiot woman on the loose, I go weak all over." He added softly: "I love you so much, darling."

She lifted her eyes. "You really mean that, don't you?"

"Of course I mean it." His tone was ragged. His arms around her tightened. "Why else would I care so much about your safety?"

And why, she wondered, did her heartbeat quicken so strangely because he did care? She trembled against him, then drew out of his arms as Cathy came in, announcing that she was ready to swallow her pills. No, she didn't feel much better. Her throat felt scratchy, and she felt kind of dizzy. "But I guess I'll feel better tomorrow," she said, smiling for Larry as he helped tuck her warmly under the covers.

But she wasn't all right the next day, or the day after that. It wasn't that her temperature rose alarmingly, or that the cold, settled in her throat and chest, showed any real danger signals.

It's as if, thought Tracy, she had lost interest in life. The more she considered that, the more it disturbed her. The eyes of a child of nine shouldn't have lost their lustre simply because she was in bed with a cold. And she shouldn't be so apathetic about everything.

She was terribly pale, thanking Larry for bathing her face, or bringing her food, or straightening her covers. For every little thing, it was: "Thank you so very much for

172

waiting on me." Or: "Oh, Tracy, I love you so much. What would I do without you?" But then the young eyes would cloud over and go back to staring dully at nothing.

Why? Because she had so much time on her hands, so little to do but keep the fire going and sit in front of it, thinking, Tracy spent a lot of time trying to figure out what was basically wrong with Cathy.

When the answer finally came to her, early Wednesday afternoon, it was simple. Cathy had had the rug pulled out from under her life. First she had lost her mother, then, so she believed, the love of her father. And there went her sense of security. Youngsters had to have someone to hold to. They needed the assurance of that person's love. Without this they were lost. And that described the look in Cathy's dull, staring eyes – the look of a child who was lost!

Thinking about this, anger grew in Tracy. A wide drape was drawn, shutting off the little alcove where Cathy was taking a nap. Tracy was alone to pace the floor and mutter aloud bitter imprecations on Bert Brooks, who had done this to a lonely, helpless child.

"The idiot!" ran her mutterings, and her teeth gritted. "And all over a lunatic blonde with an angelic face."

In her early hospital days, while she was

173

still in training, she had seen a lot of cases of men making fools of themselves over some pretty girl who caught their fancy. Sometimes it was a man patient, sometimes a doctor. She had seen plenty of it later on, too. But a nurse became more sophisticated with the years, learned to take it for granted that many men lost their wits and common sense when the wrong woman came along. Oh, she had seen plenty of that sort of thing in these last seven years.

Interrupting her own thoughts, she lit a cigarette, turned a log on the fire, put on a fresh log, then resumed her pacing and thinking.

But never before had she seen a man go so completely off his rocker as to jeopardize his professional standing, desert and neglect and abuse his own child, all for the sake of a woman who –

And then she heard Cathy's frantic scream, hysterical with fear. Turning, she saw the child stumbling toward her, and in the same split-second saw Fern Wilson walking into the room, walking toward them, smiling as she came, smiling, smiling, smiling – and pointing a small revolver at them.

"It isn't the same one I had before," she said sweetly to Tracy. "Naturally not, since you tossed that one to the birds. But this

174

one will work even better. I'll see that it does when I get around to giving it the go signal." And she kept on walking toward them.

Cathy's screaming had stopped. She stood riveted close to Tracy, like a child paralyzed, her eyes trance-like as she watched the pointed, moving weapon, forever coming closer.

"Don't be afraid, sweetheart," Fern said sweetly, almost tenderly. "It's unfortunately true, of course, you'll have to burn in the fires of hell. But you'll have me for company. I have three bullets in this little toy, and one of them I'll save for little old me. And I give you my word, after I run outside and set the world on fire, I'll run right back in and use that third bullet on my silly old head. So we'll all go together when we go, right down into the fires of hell. Won't that be fun?"

Then her laughter rang out, shrill, insane, as her finger moved on the trigger. And with a small sigh, Cathy collapsed on the floor, her face like death.

"You insane murderess!" Tracy cried, bending over the child.

"Let her alone," Fern ordered, just as the door opened and Larry walked in.

Chapter Nineteen

Even later, after it was all over, it was hard for Tracy to believe that the nightmarish moments which followed had been for real. "What's going on here?" asked Larry quietly, and moved quickly, throwing his full weight against Fern's arm, reaching for the hand which held the revolver, still aimed at Tracy. Her wrist moved, but the fingers did not release their grip. The finger on the trigger moved, moved twice. One bullet went wild; the second was a close hit in the area near Larry's heart.

Tracy screamed, "You've killed him!"

"No, it's nothing really," Larry said, trying to reassure her. But he was staggering toward the couch. And right then Cathy sprang up, unaware of the blood seeping down her arm from her right shoulder, and reached for the wrought-iron fire poker. Like a ferocious little animal, she made for the blonde girl who now, astonishingly, was seated on the floor. She was staring dazedly at the gun in her hand, now useless. "I've run out of bullets," she muttered crazily. "I've run clear out of bullets."

With both hands Cathy raised the poker and brought it down over the beautiful golden head. But her arms were not very strong, and Fern was able to spring up, clutching her head as she dashed for the door and out.

With a shrill, completely insane laugh, she cried: "Daddy, I'm on my way. You always said I'd burn in hell for being so naughty, and here I go!"

It was only a matter of seconds until the police car drove up outside. Tracy did not hear it stop, did not even hear the officer's horrific shout: "Good God, that's a human torch running into the woods!"

Later she would learn that Fern, using kerosene she had hidden outside, had set herself on fire.

Later she would learn so many things. But at the moment she was bending over Larry, trying to stanch the blood from the wound, and praying with all her might:

"God, please send help!"

That help came almost instantly and seemed at the time like a miracle.

Bert Brooks came in, looking as white as a sheet. But as he took over with Larry, examining, administering, pronouncing the wound a nasty one but safely away from the heart area, Tracy was aware of a new sense of purpose about him. Later she would decide

177

that maybe the terrific beating he had taken had made a man of Bert.

Being herself now in a mild state of shock, Tracy had to sink down on a chair as the reaction set in, and just sit there, watching as Bert went outside, called to the police officer to radio for an ambulance, then came back and went to Cathy, who was sitting patiently, as still as a little statue.

"I'm all right, Daddy," she said, as Bert got to his knees beside her, gently pulling the sleeve away from her injured arm.

She wasn't all right. The flesh wound was an ugly one, but, happily, not too serious. "This will hurt a bit, honey," Bert said, as his knowing fingers probed. "But after we get you to the hospital and get you fixed up, I'll give you something to make you sleep. In a day or so you'll be just fine."

"I'm fine now," said Cathy, determined to be brave, trying to smile.

But when he smiled back, telling her: "You're my brave little girl I love very much," Cathy gave a deep sigh, murmured, "Oh, Daddy!" And collapsed in his arms, unconscious, like a tired doll who had gone to sleep.

An hour later the ambulance arrived, then drove off with the two patients. Tracy and

Bert were following, Bert driving Larry's car.

Tracy slowly recovering from the initial shock, began to feel more like herself, although occasionally she gave herself a surreptitious pinch, just to make sure the nightmare was over and that she had nothing more to be afraid of.

Now she wanted to know exactly what had happened.

Why had Bert arrived at the cabin just when she needed help so desperately? And how had Fern known about the cottage and how to find it?

She glanced at Bert, at his grim, set face. Tracy thought: Suddenly he looks like an old man, and felt pity for him. She sensed that he shrank from talking about what he had been through in the last few hours. But she had the right to a few answers.

Finally he looked around, his eyes meeting hers, and said: "You're in love with Larry Sizer, aren't you?"

She nodded. "Yes. Yes, I suppose I am."

He drew a long, difficult breath. "I'm glad, Tracy." Then he braked the car to a stop before he repeated: "I'm glad you had sense enough this time to love a man who rates a girl as wonderful as you are."

"You seem to have changed your opinion of Larry."

"That's right. I have."

There was another silence; then he burst out: "Look, Tracy, no man likes to eat humble pie, to admit he's made a complete fool of himself over a girl who never existed!"

"Fern existed."

"No. Not the girl I adored and believed in." He shook his head, his tone bleak. "That girl was simply a figment of my imagination."

"When did you find out?" Tracy asked quietly.

"When I made the phone call to the New York hospital."

After Sunday, when Larry had, in effect, threatened him with serious trouble, Bert had gotten in touch with the head of that mental institution. As was to be expected, they would give out no information immediately. Records had to be checked, his own identity verified. All kinds of red tape had to be gone through. But finally, just this morning, he had been given the full report on Fern Wilson.

"Did it hit you hard, Bert?" Her voice was very gentle.

He thought about that for a moment. "Truthfully, no, not the way you mean." He glanced at her. "Does it make any sense if I say I felt like a man who had been critically ill over a long period, and suddenly found himself on the road to recovery?"

180

Tracy just smiled at him.

Afterwards had come the unpleasant business of having it out with Fern. First, however, he had phoned Larry Sizer, told him all that he had found out, offered his apologies, and asked if Cathy was with Tracy and where he could find them. Larry had told him, given him directions how to find the mountain cabin.

Just to make sure he had it straight, Bert had repeated the directions after him, and when he put down the phone he discovered that Fern had come in and had been standing there listening.

"So, that's how she knew where to find us," Tracy said.

"Yes." He frowned. "And that she had a chance to find you was my fault." He should never have let her leave his office without some kind of supervision. But she had gotten to her knees, pleading, weeping, imploring him to give her one more chance to prove she could live a normal life.

"And yet –" he shook his head, as if baffled by his own gullibility – "there was nothing normal about her when she first discovered I knew the whole truth."

She had, he said, reverted straight back to her early childhood, when the stern, autocratic father she had adored had held a burning match to the bottom of her foot to teach her never to play with matches.

"So that's how it all started." Tracy nodded understandingly.

"Yes. Later came the small thefts and lies she was accused of, and the warnings that she would burn in hell."

Again Tracy nodded. "All the wrong-doings that she projected onto Cathy." Then she asked him: "Did she by chance admit starting that awful hill fire?"

When he said yes, she had even boasted about it, Tracy could not help her look of shock. "And after that, you let her walk out of your office just like anybody else?"

He groaned. "Don't rub it in, Tracy. Don't you think I have enough on my conscience? Do you imagine I can ever forget that she came close to killing my own child?"

She touched his arm with great gentleness, and her eyes held only compassion. He had, she reminded, been wise enough to contact the police and come immediately.

"You must forget, Bert. Blaming yourself for something that might have happened – and luckily didn't – is all wrong. You have Cathy to think about now. Learn to be a good father, learn how to show the love I'm sure you feel for her. Love and live for your child, until some really swell girl comes along who will love and live for both of you."

An hour later, at the hospital, Tracy went to Larry's room.

His smile was wide when he saw her, but when he stretched his hand toward her she saw the bandages holding his other arm close to his body. And as she sat on the edge of his bed, she could not stop the mist of tears in her eyes, or hold her lips steady.

"Another two or three inches, and you might have been killed." There was anguish in her tone at the thought.

"But I wasn't," he reminded her, holding her hand warmly, then stroking her arm with his fingertips. "And I never was one to worry about what might have happened. If I must worry, I believe in concentrating on what may or may not happen in the future." His eyes were warm on her face.

Her concern was still for all those bandages. "Larry, are you in pain?"

"Of course not," he assured her, reminding her that he was an expert at hypnotizing pain away. He frowned. "But I can't seem to work the hypnosis bit on this worry that is driving me half out of my mind."

She laughed. "What worry is that, Larry?"

"Well –" he looked thoughtful – "let's put

183

it this way. Now that Bert Brooks has had a return to sanity, he'll be looking about for a suitable mother for little Cathy."

Tracy interrupted, "And what has that to do with me, friend?"

"Maybe nothing, maybe everything." After all, he ruminated, she would make a really wonderful mother of Cathy. And there was the matter of her long-standing obsession over Cathy's father.

"And this is what you're worrying about?"

"Well, sure. After all, sweetheart, as I've told you once, twice, maybe three times, you do happen to be the gal I've fallen in love with." He sighed. "But how can I compete with an obsessive interest in a guy with a lonely little daughter and a Hollywood profile?"

Her scowl twisted into a smile. "To start with, I never had an obsession about any man. I," she said firmly, "was simply waiting to find the man I could be obsessed about. And now that I've found him –"

"Let me get this straight," he interrupted. "Are you telling me you have found him?"

She bent down and pressed her cheek to his. "Oh, yes, yes. I've found him, darling. For all I know," she went on, her voice little more than a whisper, "he may have done a little job of hypnosis on me, because I never felt like this before, not about any man." Her lips brushed his cheek. "But whatever caused this strange feeling I have, it's wonderful."

He pulled her face around and, for a moment his eyes were lost in hers. "How wonderful?" he whispered.

She smiled at him, then straightened. "I'll tell you when you feel stronger."

"Now," he begged.

She shook her head. "You're a sick boy, remember? What kind of a nurse would I be if I said things to get you excited?"

He was still clutching her hand warmly. "You're cruel."

"No. I'm being a wise, considerate nurse."

He sighed. "Well, at least you can tell me one thing before you go, to carry me through my night of pain and suffering. Please?"

She leaned down, put her lips gently on his, and told him: "I love you, darling."

AP 4 '98